KT-381-565

APACHE RIFLES

Brick Shaftoe hurries to the town of Brass Neck in New Mexico after he receives an urgent cable from his brother. The Apache chief, Manganellis, is being supplied with guns to terrorize the smaller ranchers. Then he finds that his brother has met with a fatal accident and he believes that this is no coincidence. Brick vows to discover the truth about what has been going on in Brass Neck . . . no matter how rocky the road is along the way.

DM

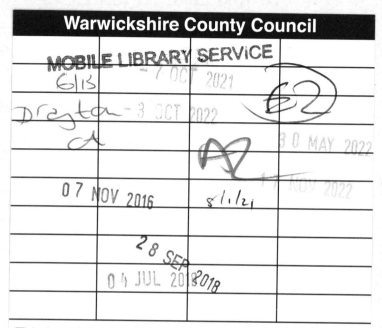
This item is to be returned or renewed before the latest date above. It may be borrowed for a further period if not in demand. **To renew your books:**

- **Phone the 24/7 Renewal Line 01926 499273 or**
- **Visit www.warwickshire.gov.uk/libraries**

Discover • Imagine • Learn • *with libraries*

Warwickshire County Council

Working for Warwickshire

ETHAN FLAGG

APACHE
RIFLES

Complete and Unabridged

LINFORD
Leicester

First published in Great Britain in 2010 by
Robert Hale Limited
London

First Linford Edition
published 2011
by arrangement with
Robert Hale Limited
London

British Library CIP Data

Flagg, Ethan.
 Apache rifles. - -
 (Linford western library)
 1. Western stories.
 2. Large type books.
 I. Title II. Series
 823.9′2–dc22

ISBN 978–1–4448–0790–5

Published by
F. A. Thorpe (Publishing)
Anstey, Leicestershire

Set by Words & Graphics Ltd.
Anstey, Leicestershire
Printed and bound in Great Britain by
T. J. International Ltd., Padstow, Cornwall

This book is printed on acid-free paper

1

Rocking the chair

The lone rider plodded wearily out of the arid badlands. His tall rangy profile shimmered under the relentless heat generated by the desert thermals. Apart from a palamino-hide vest, he was clad entirely in black. The ornately beaded garment was from Lone Wolf, a reward bestowed by the grateful Comanche chief whose young son he had saved from the voracious jaws of a hungry mountain lion.

Head drooping with fatigue, Brick Shaftoe slapped the thick coating of ochre dust from his duds. He had been on the trail for upwards of two weeks. It had been a long haul.

Locating sufficient drinking water had been the main problem. On more than one occasion he had come across springs that had become poisoned. Only the bleached bones of earlier hopefuls had saved him from a similar fate.

Reining up, Brick hawked up a lump of gritty phlegm from his parched throat before taking a sip of brackish water from the canteen. He shook it. Hardly enough left for a desert rat.

Though the change had been barely discernible, the endless sea of desiccated sagebrush and thorny mesquite had gradually surrendered to a less harsh form of landscape. Rider and horse now appeared to be entering more congenial surroundings, more in keeping with the cattle country he was used to. And not before time.

Deftly he rolled a quirley and lit up. The acrid bite of the tobacco afforded almost as much pleasure as the rapid dispersion of the persistent flies that had been his ever-present companions. Like a nagging wife, they were an irritant difficult to contain.

A dark frown creased the handsome

features as he stared glassily towards the western horizon. Reaching into his vest pocket, Brick withdrew a crumpled slip of paper. Not for the first time, he perused the enigmatic contents.

Each successive reading of the brief missive elicited a more deeply pitted frown of concern.

It had been wired from the town of Brass Neck in the south-western corner of New Mexico. A centre for the local cattle trade, the town lay to the north of an inhospitable cluster of mountains known as the Hidalgo Pyramids. It lay close to where the borders of Texas, New Mexico and Arizona converged.

Brick's older brother had been investigating the ever-increasing problem of maverick raids by the Mescaleros. Both men were special agents attached to the Indian Agency. Their job was to police the recently established reservation. It was an onerous task due to the stoic resistance and distrust of the Apaches. Like an irritating wound that would not heal, they refused to accept the white man's sullied hand of benevolence.

Manganellis in particular was especially difficult to contain. He and his bunch of renegades had somehow gotten hold of rifles and were using them against the influx of immigrants flooding into the newly opened territory. Word had filtered down the grapevine that the Apache chief had bought the firearms in exchange for gold. Old stock discarded by the army, they were still capable of wreaking havoc amongst the settlers.

The Agency had assigned Tom Shaftoe to discover from where the guns were originating and to plug the hole. Remote and inaccessible, the San Luis pass in Hidalgo was the perfect route through which such a nefarious trade could be conducted.

Brick had not heard from his brother in over two months. Then the telegraph wire had been delivered to his quarters in Dallas, Texas.

Slowly and with deliberation, Brick tugged down the wide brim of his

Stetson to shade out the lowering afternoon sun. Scanning the few lines of typescript, he once again attempted to figure out what hidden message lay behind the seemingly innocuous text.

It read:

> *New consignment of barbed wire due in from south via old pony route. Seller wants to raise the price. Others interested. Please advise how to proceed. T.*

Then it struck him. Like a bolt from the wide blue yonder, the bitter truth of the conundrum was hammered home. And it did not bode well.

Brick slammed the heel of his palm against his forehead. Why had he not thought of it before?

'Shoulda darned well known what Tom was goin' on about,' he rapped gruffly. A prairie dog snapped its head up in surprise, then quickly disappeared into its burrow. 'And there it is, staring me right in the face.'

To the unenlightened, the wire was a simple communication between business associates. But to Brick Shaftoe it was now revealed as a vital summons for help. And an urgent one too. Tom would never have sought *advice* from his younger kin had he not been desperate. A hard-bitten gunfighter experienced in the fickle ways of renegade young bucks, he could handle himself in 'most any situation. This one was clearly beyond his capability.

Reference to barbed wire must mean that guns were coming up from Mexico by a back trail to avoid any contact with the law. Brick's eyes narrowed as the full implications of the message became clear. Raising the price had to mean Tom was under suspicion from whomsoever was selling the guns to the Apaches. And he had been forced into hiding.

The younger Shaftoe shrugged off the grave mood of foreboding that threatened to consume his thoughts.

6

The sooner he reached Brass Neck, the better.

He flipped the burned-down quirley away then finished off the last few drops from the canteen.

'We ain't got time to linger,' he murmured to his horse. 'Tom needs our help bad.'

The grey mare snickered in agreement, her proud aquiline head bobbing as he kneed the horse into motion.

During the period he had been on the trail, Brick had not encountered a living soul, unless you count the odd curious buzzard hoping for a meal, along with a wide variety of lizards. He'd even caught a glimpse of that elusive character, the mysterious road runner.

But they didn't count.

Of human cameraderie, there was none. Normally a loner preferring his own company, even Brick Shaftoe would have welcomed a friendly face. Someone with whom to pass the time of day, chew the fat for a spell over a mug of Arbuckles. Shadow might be a faithful companion, but the horse was rather deficient in the conversation department.

It came as something of a shock, therefore, when his ears picked up the unaccustomed inflection of voices. The welcome sound appeared to be coming from the far side of a rock-fringed knoll some hundred yards up the trail. Ears tingling in anticipation of some repartee, he jigged the grey to a canter.

Only as he drew closer to the crest of the low rise was Brick able to ascertain that the parley was decidedly brittle, threatening even. One voice in particular was dominating the proceedings. And it was definitely raised in anger. The obvious conclusion he drew was that some contentious issue was in the process of being sorted out.

Dismounting behind the cluster of boulders, Brick removed his Winchester carbine from its saddle boot and checked the load before sidling up to the lip of the knoll. He removed his hat and peered around the side of a rock.

The sight that he beheld brought a fractious glint to the hawkish gaze.

Six men stood in a half-circle. Guns drawn, they bleakly eyed a seventh who was berating a Mexican. The object of their wrath was little more than a boy. He was clearly terrified of the hard-nosed tough who was threatening dire retribution for his having trespassed on to Rocking Chair land.

The hectoring invective was approaching its vengeful climax.

Turning to an equally thuggish confederate, the burly leader of the group snapped his fingers. Without preamble, a coiled bull whip was slapped into the outstretched palm. He shook out the writhing brown serpent to its full length of twelve feet.

'We don't take kindly to no stinkin' greaser trespassin' on our land,' he snarled, cracking the whip with ominous intent. 'And then butcherin' stock. Now ain't that the last straw, eh boys?' There was no need for any response.

But it came anyway in the form of growled imprecations.

Casually he walked across to a small fire over which a haunch of meat was roasting. With purposeful deliberation he kicked over the sizzling feast and ground it into the sand.

'Time we taught you a lesson, greaser,' he muttered.

'But I was hungry, señor,' protested the frightened youngster, trying to scuttle crablike away from the flicking tongue of the snake. But there was no escape as the circle crowded in on him. 'Not eaten for five days. And she was only a calf with broken leg. Had already died when I found her.'

The earnest plea received mocking jeers.

'That's what they all say,' spat one snake-eyed jasper.

'Is true! Is true!,' exclaimed the boy, desperation making his raised voice crackle with dread. 'No intend steal your cattle.'

'Too late for all this mealy-mouthin,

kid,' rasped the leader brusquely. 'Us Rockin' Chair rannies know exactly how to deal with scum like you.' He paused, a mirthless grin scoring his wrinkled features. 'Don't we, boys?'

'Sure do, Jug,' chorused the surrounding cohorts.

'Tie him to the trunk of that cottonwood,' ordered Jug Lassiter, who ramrodded the outfit. Ears like barn doors wagged with fervor. Some called him Jug Ears. But never to his face. One poor sucker had made that error. He now occupied a piece of real estate in Brass Neck's cemetery.

Two rannies grabbed a hold of the squirming boy and dragged him across to the tree.

'Please, please, señores. Have mercy, I beg of you.'

But the heart-rending entreaty fell on stony ground. Cold, merciless eyes followed the brutal performance. A harsh tearing of cloth exposed the bronzed back of the young Mexican.

Brick knew that he had to do

11

something. And *rapido*!

If there was one thing that stuck in his craw, it was bullying. And when the recipient was a kid, his hackles were raised. He had experienced enough of that as a kid himself at the hands of a drunken father. So all his instincts screamed out to rush down, rifle in one hand and revolver in the other, blazing away.

But seven to one were not favourable odds. He might drop two or maybe even three. But the others would surely get him.

'Damn it!' The frustrated exclamation stuck in his throat. 'What in hell's teeth am I supposed to do?'

That was when his years of experience as a law officer came to the rescue. Elbowing aside a natural born tendency towards foolhardy heroics, he forced himself to remain calm.

The wicked bullwhip rose into the static air. It hovered, a twitching serpent itching to tickle the exposed back of its prey.

Suddenly, as if plucked by the hand of some bewitching spectre, it spun away. The braided shaft had been smashed in half by an accurate .44.40 bullet from Brick's Winchester. Another well-positioned slug took the boot heel off another stocky jasper who was already bringing his own rifle to bear. Caught off balance the cowpoke fell to the ground.

Instinctively, Brick called out a warning to the men below.

'Drop your weapons and stand back!'

The command was delivered in a curt, businesslike manner. At least momentarily it had the effect of stunning the group of badgering toughs into immobility. But only for an instant.

Quickly recovering from the shocked interruption to their macabre party, Jug Lassiter swung on his heel and went for his holstered six-gun. Unfortunately for him there was no visible target. The two shots he managed to squeeze off were wildly inaccurate, ricocheting off the surrounding rocks well wide of their mark.

Brick had remained in hiding. Now he added a pointed follow-up to his previous command. A single shot from the Winchester removed the gunman's hat. His big ears flapped in alarm. The shot had parted Lassiter's greasy hair while ploughing a red furrow across his scalp. The foreman yelped, slumping to his knees while clutching at the bleeding wound.

'Anyone else moves a muscle,' Brick hollered curtly, 'and they'll be chewing on a lead sandwich.'

Then came the clever bit. To lend an air of authenticity to the illusion that he was not alone, Brick added with firm conviction, 'Keep 'em covered, Charlie, while I step down there and even up the odds somewhat. The rest of you boys spread yourselves along the ridge.'

'Sure thing, Sheriff.' Brick's reply to his own order was uttered in a gruff Kentucky lilt in contrast to his own West Texas drawl.

The main thing, though, was that the

ruse had the desired effect.

Gunbelts were unbuckled and fell to the ground. Arms rose into the air. The charade that a sheriff's posse had stumbled upon their vindictive designs had paid off.

But Brick knew that he would have to work fast. No way could he expect these jiggers to be hoodwinked indefinitely. If his spectral posse failed to appear soon, the critters would smell a rat.

Hustling down the gravel incline, he roughly slammed his boot into Jug Lassiter's backside as the thug was attempting to stand up. He had correctly surmised that the burly foreman was in charge. A pained howl broke from the bully's clenched teeth as he sprawled headlong into the dust.

'Stay on your belly like the wriggling sidewinder you are,' Brick growled ramming his boot heel into the guy's back as a harsh reminder of who was holding the aces. 'The rest of you skunks move away from them shooting irons. And keep your mitts where I can see them.'

Rifle and revolver panned the hesitant group of cowboys.

'This greaser was trespassin' on Rocking Chair land,' piped up a tall lanky dude. 'Mr Williams, the owner, don't cotton to that round these parts.'

'And he's a thief,' added another. 'Don't that deserve a whippin'?'

'Well, you can tell this Mr Williams that nobody has the right to take the law into their own hands,' replied Brick who was nervously eyeing the hovering men. It was clear that they were beginning to recover their nerve.

Hands had lowered, fists were clenching. This was no time to hang around.

'You!' He jabbed his revolver at the nearest rannie. 'Untie the kid.' Trying to stretch his luck, Brick then called out over his shoulder to the hallucinatory posse. 'If any of these critters tries any funny business, shoot him.'

Once the Mexican had been freed,

Brick said to him, 'Grab a horse, kid, and get out of here. Me and the boys will catch you up.' For a second the youngster just stood there, mesmerized, his brain unable to take in the significance of what was happening.

'*Vaya pronto, muchacho!*'

The brittle command, uttered in his own tongue, immediately spurred the boy into action.

'*Gracias, señor,*' he replied, hastening over to the tethered remuda. The tattered remnants of his white shirt flapped idly like paper wings as he hit the saddle of his own mount.

Immediately the boy had spurred off up the trail, Brick followed. A muttered grumbling pursued him as he backed up the loose slope behind.

'This guy ain't no lawdog,' snarled the lanky cowpoke known as Dutch Eddie. 'Where's his goldarned tin star?'

'And it seems to me like there ain't no posse neither,' opined a third.

'Get him, boys!' snapped Jug Lassiter who had recovered his voice.

A surging rush forward was quickly brought to a stuttering halt as Brick let fly with his .45. Orange flame spat from the bucking six-gun. One shot removed the Dutchman's little finger while the other floored a large barn door of a wrangler called Billy Gibbs. Blood spurting from a ruptured vein in the big man's thigh quickly scotched any attempt at further retaliation.

'The next bullet will be a killing shot,' rasped Brick as he nervously covered the incensed huddle. But the threat was enough to stymie any potential charge. No further difficulties were encountered as he gratefully breasted the lip of the knoll and disappeared from view.

2

Chivalry at a price

Wasting no time, Brick leapt into the saddle of the ever patient Shadow and urged the mare away from the source of danger. By the time the uninjured cowboys had recovered their guns and reached the far side of the knoll, their assailant was long gone.

Brick dug his spurs in and urged the grey to a frenzied gallop. He wanted to catch the Mexican boy up and ensure that they both reached the safety of Brass Neck unscathed.

The lawman had purposely ridden off in the opposite direction to that taken by the fleeing Mexican to prevent any pursuit of the youngster.

His aim now was to circle around and try to pick up his original trail on the far side of the recent arena of conflict. With various members of the Rocking Chair crew out of action, he surmised that they would head back to the ranch for some doctoring. Every ranch had a practical cowpoke who could fix minor injuries and set broken bones. He would be earning his pay soon enough.

After an hour of heading north, Brick swung the cayuse into the setting sun. It was a further hour before he was eventually able to rejoin the main trail. Long shadows spread their fingers across the land inexorably swallowing up cliffs of deepest orange where the sun's rays still held sway.

It was a beautiful time of day. But the Indian agent had other things on his mind. Of the young Mexican there was no sign. Perhaps he had got lost.

Scanning the trail ahead, his keen eyes searched for a suitable campsite. The recent vitriolic encounter had been relegated to a back room in his mind. But not for long. The scrabbling of rocks immediately in front of him followed by the snickering of a horse brought the incident back into full focus.

'What the heck!' he exclaimed, instinctively throwing himself out of the saddle. His immediate assumption was that the range riders had out-manoevred him and were figuring on mounting an ambush. Revolver palmed and cocked, he snapped off a couple of warning shots, the intention being to momentarily confound the bushwhackers' aim, giving him the chance to find cover.

'*Basta ya! Basta ya!*' The urgent cry to cease firing was followed by a tatty piece of torn white cloth waving from behind a boulder. 'It is I, *señor*,' called a panic-stricken voice.

Caught napping, Brick shot back with a brittle retort. 'And who in hell is that meant to be?'

'The poor *muchacho* you rescued from the beating,' came back the anxious reply. The boy had obviously assumed that his saviour would know who he was. As there had been no other Mexican travellers on the trail, Brick could only shake his head in disbelief as the truth dawned.

Tentatively the Mexican boy appeared from behind his place of concealment.

'Come out where I can see you,' ordered Brick. He was still unwilling to accept that this was not some sort of trick engineered by Jug Lassiter.

The boy emerged, shamefaced and trembling with fright.

'Anybody else hiding behind there?' snapped the Indian agent, following up with a more positive challenge, 'If there is you'd be well advised to come out now.'

'I alone, señor,' said the boy holding his hands high. 'Heard rider coming and thought it was bad cowboys.'

Cautiously, Brick stood up and came over to join the boy, not forgetting to keep his revolver primed and ready, just in case.

'Don't ever do that again, kid,' he admonished the relieved boy. 'You could have gotten yourself killed.'

'I am very sorry, señor,' he answered.

Brick responded with a caustic grunt. He angled a calculating eye towards the dipping sun before announcing, 'This seems as good a place as any to camp up for the night.' His other beady peeper fastened on to the fidgety Mexican. 'You hungry, *muchacho*?' He recalled the kid's contention that he had not eaten in five days. The kid certainly looked a scrawny mutt.

'*Sí, sí, señor*,' emphasized the boy, vigorously nodding his head. 'I not eaten for — '

'Yeah, I know,' Brick interposed. 'So how's about you set up a fire while I hook out some chow. Bacon and beans OK?' A loose smile momentarily cracked the hard features before once again reverting to a stony mask.

The boy's mouth watered at the thought of hot food as he quickly sought out some dry kindling.

A half-hour later, the two unlikely travelling companions faced each other across the flickering tendrils of the fire. An amused smirk crossed Brick's face as he watched his new *amigo* desperately shovelling the grub into his mouth like there was no tomorrow. It disappeared faster than a rat up a drainpipe.

Greedily the boy was eyeing the spare strips of bacon sizzling on a rock adjoining the fire.

'You fancy seconds?' Brick grinned. A brisk nod and the boy's hand shot out. 'You sure weren't joshing about being ravenous,' observed the Indian agent as he mopped up his own tin plate with a hunk of stale bread.

The kid's left eye twitched involuntarily. The nervous reaction was quickly spotted by Brick. It was a defect that gave him a kind of lopsided look. A nervous reaction that spoke of hard times past.

'What handle do you go by, kid?' he asked.

'Pepe Montoya Bavispe de Santiago,' the boy replied proudly.

'That's one heck of a mouthful,'

Brick smiled, shaking his head. 'Too much for me. Maybe I should just call you Wink.' Brick gave a satisfied nod. 'Wink Montoya. How does that sound?'

The boy merely shrugged. The humour of the nickname escaped him.

'My *padre* owned the Colonia Morelos hacienda. It is the largest cattle spread in Sonora Province, just over the border in Mexico. Three days would not be enough time to ride from one side to the other.'

Pride in his noble heritage was instantly replaced by a depth of anguish that surprised even an old hand like Brick Shaftoe. The boy's narrow shoulders slumped.

These were the first words that had been uttered since their first meeting over an hour before. Normally Brick would have waited for his companion to offer any further personal details. Such was the code of the West. A man's business was his own, to be propounded as he saw fit, or otherwise.

But this was a boy. And he was

clearly in some distress. Why else would he be wandering alone in this god-forsaken wilderness? So Brick felt no compunction in questioning his motives for traversing such a remote and desolate part of the territory.

He selected a fresh cigar and lit up, allowing the aromatic smoke to dribble from between pursed lips.

Piercing eyes tried to tease out undercurrents that had led to this unlikely encounter in the badlands of Hidalgo. The boy looked as though he ought to be still in school. Yet there was a hardness about him that belied the innocent exterior, a catlike wariness that spoke of experiences no youngster should have to bear.

Darkness had enfolded the small campsite in its clinging embrace. The occasional gleam of light reflected from green eyes as desert creatures hovered on the outer limits. Fire was an effective deterrent to any unwelcome guests such as coyotes and mountain lions. Low grumbles and snuffles soon faded as the interlopers sought easier prey elsewhere.

'So what gives, Wink?' Brick uttered eventually.

The boy's eyes narrowed. But he remained taciturn, continuing to chew on the last of his bacon, considering. This man had saved his hide, then shared his food with a stranger in need. Such an act of generosity deserved a corresponding hand of friendship.

The boy paused, then wiped his greasy hands on the grubby rag of his torn overalls. A blank regard replaced the uneasy accord of moments before as his mind cast back. The recall was painful, eliciting a twisted grimace. It was accompanied by the nervous twitch in the boy's left eye.

'Take your time,' murmured Brick in a more empathic tone. 'I'm a good listener.'

Then the boy launched into his story.

'My parents were on the monthly trip to deposit funds in the bank at the border town of Agua Prieta. Papa had promised to buy a new dress from the store for Mama's birthday.' The boy's small fist clenched tight. A muscle in his thin neck pulsated. 'But they never got there. A cowardly bunch of *bandidos* attacked them.'

The narrative continued with a hurried torrent of mordant invective that Brick found difficult to follow. Pepe's breathing became ragged and harsh.

'Slow down, kid,' Brick chided. 'You'll trip over yourself at this rate.'

'S-sorry, s-señor,' the boy stuttered with tears in his eyes.

'And the name's Brick,' prompted the Indian agent. 'Brick Shaftoe. It's short for Brickhill. Some English kin from way back, so they tell me.'

'Sorry . . . Brick.' The boy smiled hesitantly. 'But it is the bringing of it all back that hurts so.'

'Sure, I can understand how you feel. Just try to stay calm.'

Wink nodded, then continued at a more measured pace.

'When Papa refused to hand over the *dinero*, they shot him without a second thought.' Once again he paused, teeth clenched, eyes tight shut in a futile effort to eradicate the anguish. A vengeful hiss followed. 'Then the *bastardos* . . . used Mama . . . for their own pleasure.' He accompanied a harsh expletive by hawking a gob of spit into the embers of the fire.

'Did she . . . ?' Brick was loath to ask the obvious question. 'Did she come through it OK?' he asked gingerly.

'Some of our *vaqueros* found her three days later wandering in the desert.' The boy's crushed face conveyed a haunted look that Brick found impossible to meet. He poured a fresh mug of coffee to hide his disquiet. 'But the shame was too much for her to bear,' continued the boy. His last words emerged as little more than a tight whisper. 'She ended it all a month later.'

Following this sombre revelation, a brooding melancholy enfolded the camp.

Minutes passed before the boy felt able to resume his distraught narration.

An uncle had come east from Nogales to take over the running of the hacienda. As the oldest remaining relative, the responsibility fell on his shoulders to keep the place going until Pepe attained his majority at the age of twenty-one.

Neither he nor his elder sister Consuela had met their uncle before. At first Don Diego had been a thoughtful *patrón*, showing due consideration for their grievous loss. But that soon ended once he had gotten his feet firmly entrenched under the table.

His first action was to put Pepe to work in the fields. The boy was forced to labour from dawn til dusk like a common *peon*. Such blatant contempt for his position as nephew to the new *patrón* rankled.

Pepe managed to bear the shame and humiliation proudly. At least he knew that when he attained his majority and became the official owner of the hacienda, things would change radically.

But his uncle had other ideas.

His self-seeking ambitions did not include the young boy. At some point in the not too distant future Don Diego intended to get rid of this troublesome whelp. Eradicate him from the picture. An accident could easily be arranged.

Then, as sole remaining male relative, he would inherit the entire hacienda. Don Diego could hardly believe his good fortune.

In the meantime he would enjoy the fruits of the unexpected legacy that had so fortuitously come his way. And one of the most delightful and beautiful of those benefits stood before him now.

Consuela was more than just some dark-eyed beauty from the lower ranks. She personified the elegance and dignity of her position. Her very presence mesmerized the older man.

Spellbound, riveted by the startling allure of her voluptuous profile, he wanted her badly. A fearsome hunger glinted in the close-set beady eyes. No matter that he was her dead father's elder brother. Such trivialities counted for naught when pure, unadulterated lust reared its ugly head. Tapering fingers played through the girl's lustrous black tresses.

She made no move to resist.

'Go to my room, Consuela,' he hissed, barely able to contain his rampant ardour. 'I will be up soon. Prepare yourself as before.'

'Yes, Don Diego,' replied the girl in a flat, servile tone that lacked any hint of responsive warmth. Indeed, she struggled to keep the vile loathing of his repugnant actions under wraps. She felt totally defiled, violated.

But there was no choice.

Don Diego had made it perfectly clear what would happen to Pepe if she refused his advances.

As the boy's elder sister she felt a family responsiblity. The backbreaking chore of digging salt from the quarries was reserved for the local prison population. Such a brutally oppressive task would surely kill the frail boy. Consuela was prepared to suffer any indignity to keep her young kinsman safe until he was of age to assume his rightful position as head of the family *estado*.

It was mid-afternoon when Pepe arrived back at the ranch house. He was earlier than usual due to the ploughshare having broken. His uncle needed to sign a bill of sale for a new one to be purchased. Quickly he hustled up the back stairs to Don Diego's private quarters. Muted voices from within made him pause before knocking on the door.

His young face creased into a puzzled frown. One voice sounded like Consuela's. She appeared to be crying. The *patrón*'s harsh voice was raised in anger. What was happening here?

Pepe hid behind a large cupboard as the door opened and his sister emerged. Her clothes were torn and in disarray, her normally serene features blotchy with suppressed tears. Head bowed in shame, she quickly shuffled away. All thought of the broken ploughshare was forgotten.

So that was why he had not been sent to work in the dreaded salt pits. His sister had given herself over to the carnal desire of the very man who was supposed to be caring for them both. And all to save her brother.

A burning rage filled Pepe's whole being, an overwhelming desire for vengeance against this repulsive besmircher of his beloved sister.

Stifling any thought for the consequences, he burst into the room. Don Diego had been caught with his trousers down, literally. His mouth fell open in shock at this unwarranted intrusion into his private quarters.

'What have you done to Consuela?' snarled Pepe. His whole body trembled with rage. Nerves were stretched tight as banjo strings.

'How dare you burst in here unannounced,' ranted the blustering *patrón* hurriedly adjusting his person. 'Why are you not at work?'

'It is I who should be angered,' hissed the boy, slowly advancing on his stunned uncle. 'Disgusted at this most vile behaviour perpetrated by you, our uncle and *patrón*.' Fire gleamed in the boy's maniacal regard. There was no going back now.

'Get out!' shouted the panicking older man. 'Before I have you whipped and sent to the salt pits.'

But Pepe was beyond the point of no return. A wicked-looking knife appeared in his hand. Don Diego's frightened eyes bulged. He stumbled back a step, but tripped over a chair and sprawled on the floor.

A malicious grin cracked the livid face of the boy as he sprang forward and drove the deadly blade into the man's stomach as he tried to rise.

'Aaaaaaaagh!' screamed the *patrón* clutching at the hilt of the knife. Blood oozed from the savage wound. He sank to his knees, a look of utter amazement cloaking the ashen face. 'W-what have y-you done?' he burbled.

Witnessing the man's life force pumping out of his sliced guts brought the full horror of Pepe's brutal deed into focus.

What indeed had he done?

That said, retribution for the ruining of his sister's reputation had to be meted out. Pepe scowled. He had no regrets.

'I have carried out the actions of a dutiful brother towards a cowardly *sdico*.' He spat on the floor.

Righteous vengeance had indeed been meted out. But it meant that both he and Consuela would have to leave Colonia Morelos immediately.

Pepe rushed from the room. His immediate thought was for his sister. Even before he reached her room, the heart-rending sobs filtered down the empty passageway. Yet even under such dire circumstances, he still considered it proper to knock.

'Enter if you must,' came back the

piteous response. She thought it was Don Diego come to have his perverse way once again.

A sigh of relief escaped from the girl's lips when she perceived her brother.

Pepe wasted no time in fruitless explanations.

'We have to leave straight away,' he stuttered.

'Why?' exclaimed the startled girl. 'What is the matter? You look as though a ghost is on your tail.'

'The ghost of Don Diego,' replied Pepe. 'I think I killed him.'

'What?' the girl exclaimed, dropping the bowl of water which she always used in a futile effort to wash away her shame. It smashed on the floor, unnoticed.

'I know everything about his' — Pepe gulped hard — 'his depraved dirtying of your good name.' He breathed deeply as the dire nature of his own actions struck home before blurting out, 'I . . . I stuck a knife in the lecher. There was blood everywhere. Come, come quick. There is no time to lose. You must pack your things. The field hands will be back in two hours and we must be far away by then.'

'Where will we go?' asked a distraught Consuela.

'The Angels of Mercy at Ascension will give you refuge,' said the boy. 'Nobody can enter their convent uninvited. You will be safe with them.'

'And what of you?' persisted the worried girl, already gathering her meagre possessions together. 'Where will you go?'

'I have a strong back and a quick brain,' said the boy proudly. 'Pepe Montoya Bavispe de Santiago will always find work.'

The lofty disdain for any potential dangers he might face in striking out into the unknown concealed a fearful tightness in his guts. The future was decidedly uncertain for a young greenhorn venturing into the great beyond that lay outside the confines of the hacienda. But Pepe maintained an outwardly positive attitude for his sister's benefit.

3

Brass Neck

The boy fell silent.

That had been almost six months ago.

Pepe stared into the flickering embers of the campfire. Somewhere over to his left an owl hooted a mournful call. The creature's sombre tone matched that of the boy's own thoughtful mood.

Brick himself had not interrupted the boy's narration. Suffice it to say, he had become increasingly enthralled as the grim revelations had unfolded.

'What happened after you left the hacienda?' he asked when the boy eventually recovered his composure.

Shoulders lifted in a casual gesture.

'I headed east into Chihuahua and got work on a ranch herding cattle.'

'But why come north into New

Mexico?' asked Brick, lighting up another cigar. 'The Hidalgos are no place for a young boy on his ownsome.'

'Don Diego found out where I was hiding out,' replied the boy. 'He sent men after me.'

'So you didn't manage to kill him after all,' remarked Brick.

The boy gave a shrug. He didn't appear to care.

'I figured it wise to start a new life in a new country. And when I heard that Consuela had been sent to help with a new hospital that the Angels were opening in Brass Neck, I figured it a good place to head for.'

'Looks like we're travelling the same trail then,' observed Brick. 'How's about we string along together?'

A cheery smile broke over the boy's solemn features. 'Sounds like a good idea to me,' he agreed, accepting a mug of coffee. Then, with a wry smirk, he added, 'Partner.'

They clinked tins. Partners the unlikely duo had become. At least for the next couple of days until the boy had been safely delivered to his sister at the Angels of Mercy hospital. Brick had no intentions of being permanently saddled with a young kid in his quest for answers.

★ ★ ★

Three days later the pair caught their first sight of Brass Neck.

The town stood on a flat terrace where the Pyramid Mountains surrendered to the northern foothills. Beyond was spread out a rolling prairie of rich grassland fed by the waters of the Mimbres River. As such the secluded valley was ideal for the raising of extensive beef herds.

The town catered to the requirements of the numerous ranches that had taken advantage of such a prime location. The only thing it lacked was a railroad. The cattle had to be trailed north to the nearest railhead at Albuquerque.

Fluffy balls of cloud tempered the full heat of the noonday sun. Nonetheless, Brick was more than ready to transfer the responsibility for his unexpected compadre to the kid's sister and avail himself of a welcome schooner of cold beer. And there appeared to be numerous establishments along the wide main street willing and able to furnish his needs.

He drew to a halt outside the livery stable. The ostler was washing down a large black stallion. The animal was well-lathered and dirty. Yet even beneath the thick coating of trail dust, it was clear that the creature was a real thoroughbred.

'Mighty fine-looking piece of horse-flesh,' commented Brick.

'Sure is,' replied the ostler, pausing in his task. Bud Kelly was sweating and the interruption came as a welcome excuse to pause in his labours. Caution was etched across the wrinkled visage as he laid a wary eye on the pair of riders. 'You fellas must be new in town.'

It was a statement rather than a question.

'How d'you figure that?' enquired Brick with a quizzical frown.

'Anybody hereabouts would know that this mount belongs to Mr Chuck Williams.' The man accorded the proud creature a delicate pat on its hind quarters. 'He's of Arab stock and been specially brought in from Santa Fe. I've been instructed to deliver him in person tomorrow. And Mr Williams won't want to see a speck of dust on his new purchase.' Kelly shook his head. 'And I don't blame him. This fella musta cost a fair packet.'

Brick stiffened.

'That wouldn't be the Williams guy who operates under the Rocking Chair brand by any chance would it?' The query emerged as a brittle snap.

'One and the same,' remarked the ostler, quickly picking up on the sharp tone of the question. 'Runs the biggest spread in the south-west. You acquainted?'

'Not personally,' drawled Brick, casting his partner a warning glance to keep silent. 'Although we bumped into some of his crew on the trail.'

'Not exactly the friendliest bunch, are they?'

Brick disdained to comment. Instead he asked, 'Can you direct us to the hospital run by the Angels of Mercy?'

'Sure thing,' breezed the livery man, pointing down the street. 'Just follow your nose. It's on the western edge of town. You cain't miss it.' Like all such tradesmen, Bud Kelly was innately curious, nosy even. 'You got business up there?'

But already Brick had nudged his own mount up the street in the direction indicated by the inquisitive livery man. Wink Montoya followed behind, casting a thoughtful gaze over the burg which, he foresaw, was to be his new home. The liveryman scratched his greying scalp, shrugged, then continued with his equine ministrations.

Brass Neck was a busy town, and clearly on the upward shift. Log cabins and temporary canvas shelters were rapidly giving way to more permanent structures, many of them solid and brick-built. Even as they reached the mid-point of the thriving town, a noisy argument had attracted a crowd of curious bystanders. A group of official-looking business types were remonstrating with some old sourdough miners who objected to their tents being pulled down. A pair of snappy mutts joined in the altercation.

Further along, Brick noticed that night lights were spaced at regular intervals along either side of the main street. When a steepled church came into view around the next bend, Brick knew that he had entered a town of considerable substance. There was even a guy actually employed to remove horse droppings from the street.

But it was the building on the edge of town that interested his partner.

'There it is!' exclaimed Wink, pointing to the sprawling two-storey hospital set back off the main drag. It was surrounded by a white picket fence and boasted well-tended gardens.

'Let's hope Consuela is at home,' commented Brick, who was anxious to leave the young Mexican in the safe keeping of his sister. Much as he had come to like Wink Montoya, Brick's main priority was to find his brother. Helping Tom Shaftoe solve the problem that was manifestly bugging him was proving to be an intriguing prospect.

They drew to a halt outside the hospital's main entrance.

An elderly nurse emerged. Judging by her apparel she was clearly one of the Angels of Mercy.

'Can I help you gentlemen?' she enquired almost in a whisper.

'Is there a Sister Consuela working here?' asked Brick.

'*Auxiliary Nurse* Consuela is working in the dispensary at the moment,' said the nun, laying emphasis on the fact that Consuela had not as yet taken any vows of dedication to the order. 'If you could give me your names, I will inform her that she has visitors.'

'Just tell her that Pepe is here,' replied Brick.

'Pepe?'

'That is me, Sister,' interjected the boy. 'Consuela is my . . . erm . . . sister as well.'

The old nun's raised eyebrows indicated her surprise.

'I didn't know she had any kin,' came back the surprised comment.

There's a whole heap of stuff you don't know, madam, mused Brick. But he kept the notion under wraps.

Ten minutes passed before the door swung open and the most beautiful girl Brick had ever seen emerged from the building. His jaw dropped in stupefied wonder. He could now readily appreciate how Don Diego had become so besotted. The guy had just gone about things in the wrong way.

Wink leapt from his horse and ran

over to his sister. The two embraced, hugging each other like the long-lost kin they were. Tears ran down their cheeks as both parties came to terms with this emotional reunion.

Eventually they pulled apart.

Only then did the girl notice the other visitor. Large oval eyes, brown as old mahogany appraised the handsome stranger. Brick felt himself being sucked into the vortex of their magnetic allure.

'And who is your *compadre*, Pepe?'

Uttered with slow precision, the few words poured forth like melted butter.

'This is Brick Shaftoe,' said Pepe. 'He is my *camarada*, Consuela. He saved me from being badly beaten on the trail.'

Like liquid gems, the large eyes held Brick in their hypnotic embrace. He was speechless. It took a sharp nudge from his smiling young partner to jerk a stunned brain back to the reality of his situation. Quickly, he removed his hat.

'It seems that I owe you many thanks, *señor*,' purred the enchanting creature. She held out a delicate hand which Brick took in his own bearlike paw with infinite care. 'All we need to establish now is the reason for this visit.' She cast a puzzled regard back towards her brother.

At that moment, Brick rediscovered his own voice.

'It's a long story, *señorita*,' he mumbled. 'Maybe we could go inside and Wink here' — Brick's face assumed a ruddy texture of discomfiture — 'er sorry, Pepe can fill you in.'

The girl's regal head bowed coquettishly as she accorded them both a quizzical frown.

'The refectory is cool at this time of day,' she said brightly. 'Sister Rosetta always welcomes visitors to the hospital. I am sure that she will be only too pleased to make us some tea.' As she led the way, Consuela's next comment was addressed to her brother. 'And then you can tell me all your adventures since we last met, Pepe. Or is it Wink?'

★ ★ ★

Over an unaccustomed pot of tea, served in floral-patterned china crockery together with a slice of Sister Rosetta's home-baked apple pie, Pepe brought his sister up to date with his activities. Brick was content to remain on the sidelines. Indeed he was more than content simply to enjoy the diaphanous tones and delightful charisma of this mesmeric *señorita*.

It was only a chance remark that brought him firmly back down to terra firma.

'Shaftoe,' mused Consuela thoughtfully. 'It is an unusual name. I seem to recall the marshal talking of such a name to Doctor Menendez. Although I do not know in what capacity.'

Brick's back stiffened. A saturnine aspect clouded the strong features. Could it be that Tom had been injured in some way?

'That could have been my brother Tom,' he announced bluntly. 'Was he brought in here?'

The girl shook her head.

'You have come to Brass Neck to find your brother?' she asked.

'He sent me a wire asking for help in some matter.' Brick gulped at the realization that he was getting closer to the truth much more quickly than he had expected. Much as he would have preferred to stay and get to know this Angel of Mercy on a a more intimate footing, there was no escaping the real reason for his presence in Brass Neck. 'There's questions that need asking,' he stated firmly as he stood up to take his leave. 'And maybe this sheriff has the answers.'

'Travis Hartley is the marshal,' the girl informed him. 'His office is halfway down the main street.'

Brick nodded with sombre deliberation as he stood up.

He shook hands with the girl.

'Perhaps we can meet up again sometime when my affairs here are sorted out.'

The suggestion brought a light smile to Consuela's face.

'I would like that very much, Señor Brick.'

'And it was good to have known you too . . . Wink.' He grinned, ruffling the boy's hair. 'We made a good team, eh?'

'Sure did . . . *camarada*.'

But the ardent smile quickly slid from Pepe's face. It was replaced by a doleful expression. The thought had slipped his mind that Brass Neck was the end of the line as far as his partnership with the tall Texan was concerned. Brick Shaftoe had other things to investigate. Business that did not include a Mexican runaway.

Wink's plaintive gaze followed the broad back as Brick Shaftoe led his horse back up the street towards the marshal's office.

4

Lazy dog blues

A sharp rap on the heavy oak door produced no response. So Brick levered out his revolver and repeated the procedure with more vigour and a sight more volume. Still no reaction. He tried the latch. It gave easily, swinging open on oiled hinges.

Brick's face creased into a wary frown of disapproval. This was not the result he had expected. Being allowed to wander into a jailhouse unchallenged hinted at a less than efficient incumbent. Maybe the guy was hard of hearing, or engaged in some task at the rear of the jailhouse. But that was no excuse for leaving the office open to unhindered incursion.

'Anyone at home?' he called out.

At least this got a response, which

emanated from the cellblock.

Hustling through into the narrow corridor beyond, Brick was confronted by a prisoner rather than the officer supposedly in charge.

'If'n you're after the marshal,' declared the cell's only occupant, 'he's out back tendin' to that vegetable plot of his.' The old soak's dishevelled appearance indicated that Flapjack Turner was suffering from a desperate hangover. He slung a morose glower towards the door at the end of the corridor. 'Cares more about them prized marrows than his suffering prisoner.'

Brick nodded his thanks as he headed for the back lot.

'And, mister,' added Flapjack injecting a note of disquiet into the appeal. 'You remind that son-of-a-gun that I ain't had no breakfast. My belly's rumblin' louder than a pen full of geese.'

Brick smiled an acknowledgement as he pushed through the rear door. A well-tended garden plot with rows of vegetables faced him. Marshal Hartley, a bluff, well-rounded dude pushing fifty, had all his attention focused on a hefty green marrow. If the lawdog accorded his spouse even half of such tender care, she would be well satisfied.

Standing at the far side of the vegetable plot, Brick's presence went unnoticed. It was left for him to break into the unsavoury grunting that was being accorded to the marrow.

'Marshal Travis Hartley?' he rapped as impatience at the guy's clear obsession with his charge threatened to erupt. Instead, sarcasm prevailed. 'Would it be too forward of me to interrupt this cosy rendezvous with such a prime specimen of vegetablehood?'

Taken aback by the sudden interruption, the lawman fell over.

'Who in thunderation are you?' he railed while struggling to his feet.

Not waiting for a reply, the marshal desperately tried to recover his composure. Not to mention his seriously dented persona as a tough lawman. Bristling with overheated indignation, he squared his shoulders and drew himself up, cautiously eyeing the intruder.

'I assume this is the head office for upholding the law around here and not some flophouse that any old rannigan can push his way into?' Irony in full measure dripped from the coarse enquiry.

A nasty scowl twisted the lawman's ruddy features. Brick knew he was pushing his luck, and he felt like rattling the guy's baccy-stained teeth. But he needed information. Forcing a look of contrition into his granite exterior, he somehow managed a trite apology.

'Sorry about that, Marshal,' he said. 'But the front door was open and your prisoner pointed me in this direction.'

'Umph!' snorted Hartley, wiping wet soil down his pants. 'Well, hurry up and state your business. I'm a busy man.'

Brick couldn't resist another cutting

jibe. A caustic gaze flicked downwards, locking on to the plump marrow.

'I can see that now, Marshal.'

Hartley puffed his cheeks with churlish bluster. 'It's the county championship next month. And I aim to win first prize with this beauty.'

Brick was not impressed.

'Perhaps we could address my problem,' he snapped acidly. 'That is, if you can manage to spare some time for legal matters.'

'No need to get cranky, young fella,' Hartley remonstrated in an attempt to cool things down. 'Come into the office and we can discuss things over a glass of finest Scotch whisky.'

Brick decided there was no point in exacerbating the issue and accepted the olive branch, albeit with some reluctance.

Flapjack Turner's demand for inner sustenance received short shrift from the lawman as they returned to the outer office.

'So what's your problem . . . mister?'

enquired the marshal, splashing a generous measure of the amber nectar into a pair of glasses, one of which he handed to Brick.

'The name's Brick Shaftoe and I'm looking for my brother, Tom,' Brick replied, silently acknowledging that at least Travis Hartley had good taste in liquor. 'He came to Brass Neck hoping to clear up a problem with the Indians. I received a wire asking for help. Have you any news of a Tom Shaftoe?'

Hartley renewed his glass, then imbibed a copious gulp before answering.

'Your brother was certainly here in Brass Neck, Mr Shaftoe,' he replied somewhat gingerly. 'Although I never did discover what business he was engaged in.' The lawman paused. Another sip of whisky helped steady his nerves before continuing. 'He was brought in last week.'

'Brought in?' repeated a stunned Brick Shaftoe. 'I think you'd best explain.' A hard glint skewered the edgy lawman.

'Seems like he was found some two hours' ride west of town. It was on a section where the trail narrows to little more than six feet between the cliff face and a steep drop.' Hartley stopped, unable to continue.

'You ain't finished yet,' hissed Brick.

The marshal gulped.

'His horse must have stumbled and thrown him. Broke his neck.'

'You mean he's . . . dead?'

'I'm afraid so, Mr Shaftoe,' apologized the contrite lawman. 'It was just an accident. Coulda happened to anyone. Potrillo Gap is known for being a dangerous place.'

Brick was instantly wary.

Tom Shaftoe was, or had been, an expert horseman. He had won awards for his adroitness in equestrian skills. The chances of his being thrown were slim. Sure, he could have been unlucky, just like Hartley was suggesting. But Brick was sceptical of such a mishap. Something didn't smell right here. He intended to find out exactly what had really happened.

'Who found him?' Brick's query was delivered in a flat monotone.

'Fella by the name of Jinglebob Jones. He rides for Chuck Williams who runs the — '

'Yeah, I already know,' interjected Brick snappily. 'He runs a spread called the Rocking Chair. That guy seems to just about run everything around here.' An accusing eye settled on the lawman.

'If you're insinuating that I'm in the pocket of Chuck Williams,' bristled the irate lawdog, 'you'd be well advised to curb your tongue. Talk like that ain't welcome in Brass Neck. I regret what happened to your brother. But it was an accident, pure and simple.'

Brick sunk the last of his whisky.

'I ain't accusing anyone of anything,' he said, heading for the door. There he turned, delivering a single though forceful addendum. '*Yet!*'

The lawman scowled. This guy was trouble. Like as not to become a thorn in his side. A threat to his well-ordered life. And Travis Hartley didn't cotton to that one little bit.

Brick headed across the street to the nearest saloon. He had need of more liquid sustenance to ponder over the hard fact that his brother was strumming with the angels. And not those down the street. The Lazy Dog was just one of innumerable such establishments burgeoning along the main street.

He mounted the boardwalk and was immediately confronted by the reasoning behind the saloon's colourful appendage. A large bloodhound lay splayed across the entrance. It raised a sleepy head, eyeing the newcomer with a dolorous expression.

Brick couldn't restrain a brief smile as he stepped over the torpid obstacle. Inside, the pungent odour of stale beer mingled with that of unwashed bodies. Agile couples in the centre of the room jigged to the energetic accompaniment of a pianist hammering out the latest popular air. Sunlight beaming through the open door emphasized motes of dust floating in the smoky atmosphere. Everything contributed to an atmosphere of wanton abandon.

Wrinkling his nose in distaste, Brick moved across to the bar and ordered a beer. After taking a nip of the foaming brew, he shifted along to the end of the bar to mull over recent events.

A half-hour later when he was well into his second glass, the batwing doors burst open. A noisy throng of cowboys entered. Slapping the trail dust from their duds, they swaggered over to the bar. Nobody paid any heed to the lone drinker at the far end.

But Brick was more observant. In order to remain incognito, he tugged his hat down after recognizing the spare form of Dutch Eddie. The cowpoke's right hand was sporting a bandage where his little finger had once been. A further quick glance revealed that the others had also been party to the confrontation on the trail. Frank Calder and Mac Doolin were discussing the whereabouts of one of their sidekicks.

'Where did Jinglebob disappear to?' asked Calder, downing half of his beer in one slurp. 'Last I saw of him was on the edge of town.'

Doolin uttered a manic chuckle.

'Where d'yuh think?' he scoffed, lighting up a black cheroot. 'Can't keep his gropin' hands off'n that piece of skirt he's cottoned to. The poor sap reckons he can make a decent woman of her.'

Another rannie joined in the general hilarity.

'I saw them arm in arm headin' for the Good Luck diner,' commented a bulky jigger called Denver Blue. 'Couldn't miss them shiny jinglers.'

'Yeah!' agreed Doolin. 'He was polishin' them suckers all last night.'

'You figure he's gonna pop the question?' asked Dutch Eddie, struggling with his drink on account of the thick bandage.

But he never received a reply.

Doolin nudged him in the ribs,

gesturing silently to the lone figure at the end of the bar. The bartender had broken into the idle chatter by asking the stranger if he wanted another refill.

Brick raised his head at the wrong moment.

'Well, lookee here, boys,' remarked Dutch Eddie. 'If it ain't the lowdown skunk what done for my pinkie.' He shook the injured hand at the object of his disdain. 'He needs teachin' a lesson.'

'And this time there ain't no imaginary posse to back his hand,' snarled Denver Blue. It had been his best buddy whom Brick had shot in the leg. 'Billy's gonna be out of action for over a month on account of you, lunkhead.'

'And the boss won't pay while he's recoverin',' added Doolin, pushing himself off the bar while loosening his hogleg.

Brick knew that he stood no chance of getting out of the Lazy Dog unscathed unless he did something quickly.

Without thinking he grabbed the injured Dutchman who had moved forward in his eagerness to challenge the object of his contempt. Too closely, as it happened. With one arm slung round the cowboy's neck, Brick jabbed his revolver into the fellow's back.

Silence had fallen over the other inmates of the Lazy Dog.

Dancers and the other drinkers scuttled out of the potential line of fire. All eyes centred on the violent face-off being played out. Most were used to such encounters. But they never ceased to be an arousing interlude in an otherwise mundane life. Especially when someone else's life was on the line.

'I'm leaving here,' Brick rapped in a brisk no-nonsense bite. 'Anyone tries to stop me and this guy gets a bellyful.' Gingerly he backed towards a door at the rear of the saloon.

The Rocking Chair crew followed cautiously. Flexing hands hovered above gun butts, but remained in suspension.

'Don't give him any excuse to plug me,' croaked Dutch Eddie, his bulging orbs pleading for his buddies to hold off any retaliation.

At the foot of the stairs leading to the upper floor, Brick paused, nerves strung tighter than a whore's corset. His acute hearing had picked up an alien sound. A sort of metallic tinkling. In the tense silence it was all the more poignant. A dark eyebrow furrowed.

That was when a thunderbolt struck him.

Jinglebob Jones!

The critter must have been upstairs attempting to persuade his girl in time-honoured fashion. He must have heard the commotion made by his sidekicks down in the bar — and wondered what all the ruckus was about.

Now he was clearly fixed on pushing the showdown back in favour of the Rocking Chair. An immediate response was called for.

Brick raised his boot and propelled

the helpless bulk of Dutch Eddie towards his hovering confederates. Pitched into the steadily advancing crew, the whole bunch of them were thrown into disarray. Brick swivelled and fired from the hip, emptying his pistol towards the skulking Lothario on the balcony.

Only one of the shots found its mark. It was enough. Jones threw up his arms and plunged through the flimsy balustrade. Crashing to the floor in a cacophany of jangling discords, his body lay splayed across the ancient piano. If hot lead hadn't done for the cowpoke, the fall certainly had. And judging by the glassy stare now surveying the carnage, Jinglebob Jones had forfeited his chance to walk down the aisle.

No time was wasted on surveying the outcome of his gunplay as Brick ran for the back door. Disappearing down the alley, he headed west dodging behind the chaotic huddle of buildings and vacant lots. His only thought was to thwart any pursuit. A raucous hollering informed him that the Rocking Chair boys had dispensed with any notion of seeking due legal process and were on his tail. Emerging from a narrow passageway, Brick found himself close to the hospital.

5

Dancing with the Devil

'Over here, Señor Shaftoe,' a silky voice called from an open upstairs window away to his left. It was Consuela Montoya. She had obviously heard the commotion and had a better view of the proceedings from her elevated position. She pointed to the door immediately below the window.

A raised hand informed her that the hunted man understood.

He dashed for the safe haven and disappeared inside seconds before the leading pursuer scooted round the corner. It was Dutch Eddie. The injured hand certainly hadn't affected his fleetness of foot: a trait not normally seen in cowboys. Clearly the double dose of humiliation from the vexatious stranger had lent him an added fillip.

'Where's the bastard gone?' he yelled in exasperation.

Brick sucked in deep lungfuls of air behind the closed door, a mere ten feet from the seething group of cowboys.

'Must be around here some place,' opined Mac Doolin.

'Maybe he went the other way,' added Denver Blue with a sigh. 'Could be anywhere by now.'

Dutch seethed and ranted for five minutes, his frustration barely under control. It was the sheriff who brought a halt to any further notion the group might have entertained regarding summary retribution.

'You boys get back to the ranch,' ordered Hartley. 'Let the law deal with this. If there's a case to answer, I'll make sure the culprit is brought to justice.'

Mutterings and veiled threats followed the marshal's declaration.

Dutch Eddie was less than convinced. 'When I catch up with the skunk, he's crow bait,' he snarled, ignoring Hartley's words.

The biting invective was a challenge to the lawman's authority.

Hartley's grip tightened on the Loomis shotgun. He might be a gardener in his spare time, but in no way did he lack courage.

'Nobody takes the law into their own hands in Brass Neck,' he informed the indignant rannigans. 'You'd be well advised to let me handle it. That way justice will be well served.'

The lawman's rigid stance impressed Brick, whose pounding heart-rate had thankfully returned to normal. Behind he could hear the tense breathing of Consuela, the warmth of her nearness threatening to unhinge his concentration.

'It better be,' rasped Frank Calder. 'Jug Lassiter ain't gonna be too pleased at another of his crew being shot up.'

'And Jinglebob was killed,' added Doolin. 'This will be a hangin' matter.'

'And so it will,' agreed Hartley, 'if Shaftoe caused the shooting.' He didn't wait for any more dissension. The shotgun lifted, its long twin barrels pointing ominously towards the group. 'Now go on home.'

A heavy silence settled over the grim scene.

Then, slowly and somewhat reluctantly the group of indignant cowboys dispersed.

It was another two minutes before Consuela broke the silence.

'What happened, Señor Shaftoe?' she asked, guiding him down the hallway into a small kitchen. 'You appear to have made more than your share of enemies in the short time you have been here.'

'Seeing as how we keep meeting up like this, perhaps you should call me Brick,' he said with a smile, accepting the proffered cup of coffee. 'After all, we ain't strangers no more.'

Consuela laughingly concurred with a dainty nod of the head.

Brick then went on to explain how he had been minding his own business in the saloon. The cowhands had given him no option but to fight back. It was just bad luck that a man had been killed. But it was self-defence, and the other witnesses in the Lazy Dog would surely support that contention.

'Have you somewhere to stay in Brass Neck?' enquired Consuela, accepting the handsome stranger's account without question.

Brick shook his head. Events had raced ahead of such mundane considerations.

'I have a spare room you could use,' the girl offered. Then she hurried on: 'as a paying guest, of course. I am sure you agree that a girl cannot be too careful. Her reputation . . . '

'Of course,' agreed Brick coyly. 'And I might not be too welcome at the hotel . . . under the circumstances.' Then, rather sheepishly, he added, 'This sure wasn't the way I had intended for us to become better acquainted, Consuela. Me being chased by a pack of angry hornets wanting blood.'

'You helped Pepe, so is only right

that I return favour.' Her large oval eyes seemed to gaze deep into the young man's soul. Stumped for any meaningful response, he merely grunted some banal utterance.

★　★　★

Next morning he decided to pay another visit to the marshal and apprise him of the real facts behind the killing of Jinglebob Jones. After all, he had done nothing wrong. It was self-defence. Even the narrow-minded lawdog couldn't hold him on a charge of murder.

When Brick went to see Travis Hartley in his office, the lawman had already spoken to the bartender and a couple of other witnesses. All were willing to testify that the Rocking Chair boys had started the affray and that Shaftoe had little choice but to defend himself when Jinglebob Jones had tried to backshoot him.

'Seems like you're in the clear, mister,' grunted the marshal. He appeared to be somewhat miffed at having to forgo the prospect of overseeing a murder investigation. 'But I would advise you not to hang around these parts if'n you value your health. Them boys ain't gonna take this lying down. You can bet on it. And I won't always be on hand to save your hide.'

'So there'll be no charges?'

Hartley offered a surly nod of assent.

'You don't seem too pleased, Marshal.' Brick smirked. 'Couldn't have anything to do with the hefty trial fee you'll be missing out on, I suppose?'

Hartley bristled with indignation. His florid visage creased in a sneer.

'Clear out of here, Shaftoe, before I run you in. Spitting in the street for starters.'

'All right, all right,' replied Brick quickly holding his hands up to pacify the irate lawman. 'Didn't mean nothing. Just one more question, then I'll hit the trail.'

Hartley levered up a questioning eyebrow.

'Did someone bring in my brother's horse and gear?' Brick said. 'I need to take something back to the folks in Texas.'

The marshal's tense demeanour eased, the tight expression softening. After all, the guy had lost a brother. And been set upon for helping that kid out. He deserved some measure of sympathy. Just so long as he left town afterwards.

'Go see the livery man, Bud Kelly,' suggested the lawdog. 'He's holding on to your brother's effects. Tell him I said you can have them.'

'One more thing,' posed Brick. The granite expression was solemn, as if the weight of the world was resting on his broad shoulders.

Hartley waited. His surly demeanour registered impatience.

'Where do I find my brother?'

The marshal's eyes lifted. 'He's buried in the municipal cemetery. You'll find it on the north side of town. We ain't had time to erect no gravestone yet.' Hartley's pinched visage marked the closest approximation to an apology he had thus far offered.

'Much obliged, Marshal.' Brick nodded. 'Don't worry about the headstone. I'll sort it out with the undertaker.' He stopped in mid-stride, turned and gave the lawman a sly wink. 'As for leaving town, I wouldn't hold your breath.'

The grave was on the far side of the cemetery. He was the only visitor, a situation that he welcomed. Nobody was there to witness the tears welling in his bloodshot eyes as he peered at the raised heap of bare earth. Removing his hat, the young man stood there, silent and despondent.

Clouds had amassed overhead. Stark banks of grey that heralded an imminent downpour. The dark shadows blotting out the sun matched the solitary mourner's spirit of melancholy. Here in this lonely patch of land where only the dead held sway, he had never felt so alone.

Tom Shaftoe had always been a

guiding light, a beacon of hope to his younger sibling. Since their ne'er-do-well of a father had been shot to death following a rigged poker game, Tom had been the mainstay of the family. The elder Shaftoe had hunted down the miscreants and exacted his own personal form of justice. What that amounted to had never been revealed, and Brick had never asked. Now he would never know.

Their mother had gone to pieces, retreating into a shell from which she never emerged. She lasted barely a year before dying from unspecified causes. A broken heart has never been recognized as a medical condition.

The two boys had sold up their farm in Kentucky and headed West.

A twittering cactus wren broke into Brick's sombre reverie. The tiny bird's carefree warbling brought a cynical smirk to the ashen complexion. Oh, that life could be that simple.

But it wasn't. A hard resolve flattened out the taut lines of tension that had threatened to drown him in an ocean of self-pity. There was work to be done. Brick Shaftoe would finish the task that his brother had begun.

Or die trying.

★ ★ ★

'Anybody at home?' a voice called at the open doorway of the livery stable. Brick was having difficulty reconciling the death of his brother with the belligerent attitude of the Rocking Chair spread. They seemed hell-bent on trouble, and he was stuck right there in the middle.

A man came round the corner of the barn mounted on the black stallion he had been cleaning up the day before. All the pristine qualities of the animal were now displayed to perfection.

Brick emitted a whistle of approval, remarking, 'You sure done a fine job on him, Bud.'

'Yep!' The ostler grinned, pleased with the commendation. 'I'm off to deliver him to Mr Williams.'

'Before you go,' pressed Brick, 'the Sheriff tells me you're holding on to Tom Shaftoe's horse and gear.'

'That's right.'

'Mind if'n I take a look?'

Bud Kelly frowned. What did this guy want with a dead man's effects?

'Any particular reason?' came back the suspicious query.

Brick fixed him with a sombre yet trenchant glare.

'He is . . . or was, my brother.'

Kelly swallowed. His thin face registered surprise tinged with a modicum of sympathy.

'It's the paint mare in the end stall.' A finger pointed vaguely in the general direction. 'Just shut the door when you're done.'

Without another word Kelly nudged the black out of the corral, casting a last perplexed look at the mysterious stranger.

The paint was idly munching on some fresh oats. Slung over the stall's side panel was the saddle and a full set of leathers. A painstaking examination followed. It was only towards the end that the grim discovery was made. Tight-lipped, Brick's face assumed a stony expression.

A festering anger seeped from every pore of his being as he stared down at the broad leather cinch clutched in his hands. It was frayed and well worn, appearing to the casual eye as if it had worn through, causing the saddle to slip and thus unseat the rider.

But to the more practised observer it was clear that the cinch had been cut and on the underside, to evade a general inspection. Just enough to enable the rider to get well on his way before the strands parted.

And that point had been two hours later while Tom Shaftoe was negotiating the infamous Potrillo Gap. Brick's knuckles whitened as he gripped the cinch. Thin lips drew back to reveal a macabre smile. But there was no levity in the evil grimace.

So that was how the murdering skunk had gotten rid of his brother. The rat had no doubt followed to ensure that his heinous task was duly completed. Brick knew that he had to see for himself where Tom had met his untimely demise.

Grim-faced, eyes sunk deep into their sockets, he mounted up and headed back along the main street.

But his presence had not gone unnoticed.

A certain saloon bum, only latterly released from jail, had kept his ears open during his temporary residence. Flapjack Turner pushed back his battered hat and leaned on the mop. He might be the town drunk, but Flapjack knew how to twist something to his advantage. And Jug Lassiter would pay well for what the devious critter had earwigged in the jailhouse.

For once the drunk's sozzled brain was functioning at a steady jog, hitting the right notes. The guy was heading west, and at a brisk canter. Turner quickly surmised that he could only be heading for one place.

If he set off immediately, the swamper figured, he had ample time to ride over to the Rocking Chair and warn Lassiter. The crew would then have no difficulty reaching Potrillo Gap before the stranger. And no doubt set up a surprise welcome party.

A guilty conscience had never troubled Flapjack Turner. His mind was focused on the five-star bottle of Scotch whisky the information would buy. And that was worth any amount of skulduggery.

★   ★   ★

Early afternoon found Brick approaching the allegedly notorious site of his brother's ambiguous death. He examined it closely. Sure the Gap needed care when being negotiated at its narrowest point. But if he could manage it without mishap, Tom would certainly have experienced no difficulties.

Brick furrowed his brow in thought. He was now convinced that the severed cinch was the cause of the 'accident'. The killer had hoped that his skulking duplicity would go unnoticed.

Well, he had failed.

Tom Shaftoe had been rubbed out because he had learned too much regarding the source of the smuggled rifles. That much was clear. The Apache renegades must have latched on to a local supplier. And Brick intended to find out who the dirty skunk was and bring him to justice.

Musing on how that end could be achieved, Brick failed to observe that he had been hemmed in by six riders. The realization came as a brutal shock when a lariat dropped over his shoulders dragging tight across his chest. A sharp tug and he crashed to the ground.

'Get this varmint on his feet and over to that tree yonder.'

The brusque command was followed by the dazed captive being unceremoniously hauled across to a desiccated cottonwood. Here he came face to face with the sneering visage of Jug Lassiter. The ranch foreman was standing beside the trunk, legs apart, hands on hips.

More startling, however, was the noosed rope swinging ominously in the gentle breeze. And it was obvious who was about to make its acquaintance. Two men gripped Brick by the arms.

He had been in many precarious situations during his brief life, but this was the most critical. Unless a miracle occurred in the next few minutes, he was buzzard bait.

'You've caused no end of trouble since coming to this territory,' growled Lassiter, poking his jutting snout to within inches of his victim's ashen face. 'I've got to bury a man on account of you, mister.' The sour odour of bad breath and whiskey made Brick gag. But that was the least of his worries. All the same, he couldn't resist hawking a mouthful of spittle into the leering mush.

Lassiter staggered back, wiping the

mess from his stubbled jaw.

'Lousy bastard!' he yelled, accompanying the gruff retort with a cutting backhander. The heavy blow had all the foreman's weight behind it. Brick would have ended up chewing dust had he not been held firmly between Mac Doolin and Denver Blue. Blood dribbled from the smashed mouth.

'Where we come from, it's an eye for an eye,' butted in Dutch Eddie. 'And I aim to see you pay the full penalty, Mex lover.'

'Enough of this talk,' rapped Lassiter. 'Tie his hands behind his back and get him on his horse. We got us a hangin' to perform.'

Muttered growls of agreement followed the grim announcement.

'You'll never get away with it,' spluttered Brick from between swollen lips. 'The law will hunt you down.'

Lassiter emitted a hearty guffaw.

'Don't think that our good Marshal Hartley will overtax his lazy butt,' he hissed. 'That knucklehead's jurisdiction ends at the town boundary. See you in Hell, turkey!'

And with that final ejaculation, the foreman slapped the grey's rump. The horse jumped forward, leaving Brick dancing with the Devil.

6

Back from the brink

Secreted behind a cluster of rocks some fifty yards from the site of the macabre execution, Wink Montoya gasped. A cry of anguish issued from his gaping mouth. Only distance prevented the bushwhackers from sensing his presence as sweating hands were wrung with frustration.

He had seen Brick leave town and desperately wanted to join up with him. Partners once again. Only the fear of being sent back to Brass Neck had made him hang back. Perhaps he could make his presence felt when the man took a breather. When Brick had stopped at Potrillo Gap, it seemed that Lady Luck was sitting on his shoulder.

Then those cowboys had grabbed him. Wink felt helpless, impotent with suppressed fury.

Much as he craved to rush out and save his partner, the boy knew that he would likely end up suffering the same fate. He had no weapon. And what could a mere boy do against six hard-bitten toughs? A feeling of total uselessness suffused his spare frame.

Watching the Indian agent kicking his life away on the end of a rope was more than the youngster could bear. Tears ran down his swarthy cheeks. Head in hands, he sank down and wept uncontrollably.

It was only the thunder of hoofs passing close to where he lay concealed that brought Wink back from the torment of despair. Peering out from his hideout he saw the gang of killers disappearing along the draw. They had plainly not waited to oversee the gruesome results of their deadly act. Few people passed this way. And the gang clearly didn't expect a Good Samaritan to happen along.

Wink sucked in a deep breath of hot

air. His eyes bulged. The nervous tic became more pronounced than ever. Now he might have the chance to repay his saviour. If only he could get down there and release him.

Thoughtless as to his own safety, Wink stumbled headlong down the stone-choked gully to retrieve his own cayuse. Racing across the intervening stretch of open ground, he dragged out a pocket knife and hacked desperately at the thick hemp above the deadly noose.

Brick's eyes were closed. His tongue, now little more than a purple hunk of gristle, hung out of the bloody orifice that was his mouth. The desperate thrashing had ceased. All signs of life appeared to have deserted the swaying body as it tumbled to the ground. Wink retrieved his water bottle and splashed the tepid liquid over the bloodless face. Still no movement. He leaned over the splayed-out corpse, his head bent low, listening for any sign of a heartbeat.

'Looks like we've caught ourselves a

murdering thief, Martha.'

The gruff voice made Wink jump.

Consumed by his grief, the boy had failed to heed the approach of the wagon and four. A large big-boned man now stood over him, glowering angrily. In his large meaty right hand was a Navy Colt, cocked and ready for use. Dark, hooded eyes shot daggers of hate at the supposed killer.

Standing on the wagon bed, a young woman clutched hold of a twelve-bore. Both of the newcomers looked well capable of blasting Wink into the hereafter.

The boy fell back.

'This not what it seems,' he blurted out, desperate to apprise the pair of the truth of the matter. 'This fellow my *amigo*. Bushwhackers ambush and hang him.' He pointed a trembling finger at the swaying rope and the severed noose still clamped around Brick's neck. 'I could do nothing. Not armed. See!' He lifted his arms.

'Step away, Mex,' growled the man.

His thick grey moustache twitched as he took a menacing step forward. 'While I take a look-see.' He turned to the girl. 'Keep him covered, Martha. One false move and let the skunk have both barrels.'

'Sure thing, Pa,' answered the girl with firm resolve. Her slim form stiffened as she snapped back the twin hammers, adding warily 'Is he dead?'

That was when the 'corpse' decided to postpone a meeting with the grim reaper. A husky cough was followed by a strangled moan of pain.

'Señor Brick! Señor Brick!' howled the boy.

Ignoring the warning to stand back, he rushed over to his erstwhile partner, dribbling more water into the parched mouth.

Martha Sackett lay down her shotgun and jumped off the wagon. She ran across the intervening sandy stretch, tumbled the boy aside and cradled the injured man in her arms.

Saying nothing she removed the

constricting noose, then addressed her father. 'The medical kit, Pa, before this guy pegs out.'

Joe Sackett knew better than to argue with the feisty young girl. Since her mother had died the previous year from the fever, Martha had taken control of the domestic chores on their cattle ranch. The Bar S was one of a half-dozen smaller concerns that had prospered in Hidalgo.

The pair had been to Brass Neck for the monthly purchase of supplies and had been on their way back to the ranch. It was only another hour's ride over the foothills and down into the next valley. Fortune had indeed favoured the casualty, as it was an isolated spot with no other spreads on this side of the mountains. The nearest was Buckweed Jackson's Box J on the Otero Flats some two hours to the north-east.

Brick's eyes remained shut. He was clearly in a bad way and needed care and attention. Living in such a lonesome situation meant that Martha Sackett was well versed in all manner of medical remedies. The stocky figure of Joe Sackett lifted the injured man into the bed of the wagon as if he were nought but a sack of feathers.

Wink Montoya had been forgotten. It was clear that he had been telling the truth. But there was still the matter of why such a brutal termination had been undertaken. And who were the culprits?

'You come along with us, kid,' ordered the bluff rancher. 'You can tell us all about this on the way to the ranch.'

The old rancher and the boy sat up front while Martha tended to her patient.

* * *

For two days it was touch and go. Would the tall stranger recover? That was the question Joe Sackett kept asking his daughter. Martha could only hope and pray that her ministrations would work.

Even when he showed signs of recovery Brick was unable to voice his thoughts. Only his eyes spoke of the turmoil that was raging inside. It was a full week before the tortured vocal cords resolved themselves into some form of comprehensible meaning.

Wink filled them in with the details of how their patient had come to be involved in this sorry mess. He blamed himself for everything. If Brick Shaftoe had not stopped to help him, none of this would have occurred.

'Weren't your fault, kid,' stressed the rancher once he had been told the full story. 'Them Rocking Chair bully boys have a lot to answer for. Think they can buffalo us smaller ranchers off the land. Some of us have already sold up and left.'

Joe Sackett slammed a bunched fist into the palm of his beefy hand. 'Well, they don't frighten me. No way is that skunk Williams gonna run us off this spread.' His eyes blazed with the rabid fire of stubborn determination.

Wink had offered to help out on the ranch during Brick's convalescence. He was a willing and able hand, such that after a couple of days Joe Sackett offered him a permanent job. Wink was overjoyed. His delight was doubly boosted when he learned that Brick had spoken his first words.

Martha was at his bedside, applying a soothing balm to his savaged neck where the noose had chafed. The wound was healing well but would leave a livid scar.

'Have I gone to Heaven?'

The rasping croak brought a smile to the girl's elfin face.

'Not quite yet awhile,' she grinned back. 'Just the home of Joe Sackett, owner of the Bar S ranch.'

'Thought I must be in some sort of paradise with such a pretty creature looking after me.'

Martha's oval face blushed a deep red.

'The Sisters of Mercy tell me that all patients think that about their nurses,' she replied, affecting a ready laugh that shrugged aside the unexpected though no less welcome compliment. 'Perhaps you could inform me as to whom I am attending?'

'The name's Brick Shaftoe, late of Dallas, Texas.'

The girl stiffened. Her mouth fell open as she stared at the handsome stranger.

'Sh-Shaftoe, you say?' she stuttered nervously. The Mexican boy had only ever referred to him as Brick.

The patient frowned. 'Something wrong with that, miss?'

Martha stood and paced the room before answering. Tremulously, she plucked at a stray lock of auburn hair.

'Any relation to . . . to Tom Shaftoe, the Indian agent?' she whispered. The catch in her throat hinted at more than mere curiosity.

'He was my brother,' said Brick. 'I came here at his request. But I've since learned that he was killed. The marshal reckoned it was an accident but I found out that his saddle leathers had been cut. Somebody wanted Tom out of the picture. And now the Rocking Chair want to get rid of me as well.' His hand strayed to the rough scar that ringed his neck.

'Do you think they had something to do with Tom's death?' Martha enquired.

Brick considered the suggestion before raising a puzzled eyebrow.

'I don't know,' he admitted. 'On the face of it, the two incidents don't seem connected. Them fellas wanted revenge on me for spoiling their fun with Wink, then shooting one of their buddies. But I wouldn't put anything past those critters.' Peering closely at the girl, he then posed the pertinent question. 'Did you know Tom?'

A tear etched a trail down Martha's pale cheek. She almost choked on the words of her reply.

'He was my fiancé,' she sobbed. 'We

were to be married in the fall. And now he's dead.'

Brick levered himself on to one elbow. He examined the girl with a fresh interest. Beneath the drab grey of her work clothes, Martha Sackett appeared quite trim. Rather plain of appearance, her sharp features were encased in a severe bun tied back in a black ribbon.

Not unattractive to the eye, but not Brick's type. *That* lady was back in Brass Neck, doubtless engaged in similar duties at the Angels of Mercy hospital. Although he could readily appreciate why Tom had been smitten.

'I'm sorry,' he said, equally surprised at her disclosure. It was now more vital than ever that he should find the killers. 'Did Tom say what he'd found out?'

'Only that it involved the supply of guns to the Apache renegades who have been plaguing the area,' Martha replied in a daze. 'So far they haven't touched us. But Pa reckons it's only a matter of time.'

She paused as the full import of Brick's revelation struck home. Her eyes took on a glint of fire. A new fervour of stoic determination infiltrated her whole being. 'Now that I know Tom's death was no accident, I want to help all I can to avenge his death. Have you any ideas?'

His response was an unwitting shrug.

'Only that it has to be somebody round here who knows his way around the territory,' he averred forcefully. 'Why else would they get rid of Tom and make it look like an accident? There's just one thing I can't figure.'

Martha waited expectantly.

'Somebody wants to drive the ranchers out of this valley and blame it on the Apache.' His eyes narrowed to thin slits, brows knitting in thought. 'The question is, why? There's water and land aplenty for all.'

Martha Sackett did not have the answer. And her first thought was for the welfare of her dead fiancé's brother. Plumping his pillows, she settled the injured man down.

'No point trying to work that riddle out until you're fully recovered,' she said. 'What you need is rest and plenty of it.'

It was a further two days before Brick was allowed out of bed. The brush with death had left him drained and lethargic. Martha only allowed him to take a ride around the spread after he had pestered her sufficiently.

'But don't you go tiring yourself out,' she admonished the reluctant patient.

He had just returned to the ranch when Joe Sackett hailed him. Brick nudged the horse over to where the rancher was mending a fence.

'While you were out,' he informed Brick, 'I had Buckweed Jackson over. He's holding a meeting of the small ranchers at his place tomorrow afternoon. Another spread was burned out last week.'

'Anybody hurt?' asked Brick.

'Not as far as I know,' replied Sackett. 'But Jubal Kennedy's pulling out. And I know for a fact, he wouldn't have given up without a fight.' Gritting his teeth, the rancher continued, 'These raids are getting too darned serious for us to handle independently. We need help. And seeing as how you're a troubleshooter for the Indian agency, I was wondering if'n you'd come along and address the meeting? Give your views on how we can tackle it.' The rancher eyed his guest expectantly. 'What d'you reckon?'

'Sure thing.' Brick smiled as he unsaddled Shadow. 'Be glad to. Maybe, between us, we can also figure out who killed my brother.'

7

Unwelcome Guests

There were five other ranchers gathered together in the barn besides Joe Sackett. Buckweed Jackson's wife Maisy handed out welcome glasses of her home-made lemonade together with a selection of freshly baked biscuits. They were still warm from the oven.

'You sure are one lucky dude, Buckweed,' commented a rangy guy called Hank Marlow. 'Fella could do a sight worse than have a gal like Maisy looking to his needs.' The rather plain middle-aged woman blushed at the unfamiliar compliment.

Marlow was a bachelor.

'Ain't it about time you was getting yourself hitched?' called out Monk Regan, imbibing a noisy slurp of the tasty beverage. The circular bald patch that had given the rancher his nickname glistened in the sunrays beaming in through the open door.

'Who'd marry that ugly cuss?' scoffed Howie Brandle.

'At least I walk proper,' countered Marlow, with spirit. He was referring to Brandle's bow-legged posture, the result of a lifetime in the saddle.

The others chuckled uproariously as the good-natured banter shifted.

It was Jackson who brought the meeting to order, reminding the group of the reason for their gathering.

A sombre tone descended over the worried ranchers as they sat down on bales of straw.

'We all know why this meeting has been called,' began their host. 'The Indians are on the rampage. And between us, we have to figure out some way of stopping them before any more of us are burned out.' Jackson's hooded gaze surveyed the tense faces. 'Has anybody got any ideas?'

For a long minute, nobody spoke.

Then Joe Sackett stood up.

'You all know that my daughter was betrothed to the new Indian agent.' The rancher's voice was flat, the measured statement uttered in a hollow monotone. 'And that he was killed on account of his having found out something. But we don't know what that something amounted to.' He paused to draw breath. 'But, like as not, it concerned these raids by the Apache bucks. And there's something else you don't know,' continued Sackett. 'Tom Shaftoe had a younger brother, another deputy employed by the Indian Agency. And he received a wire from Tom urging him to come out here from Texas to help sort out the problem.'

Sackett untied his necker and wiped the sweat from his brow before continuing. 'Brick Shaftoe is here with us today, boys.' Sackett threw a proud grin towards the young man. 'And we can only hope that he offers a suggestion as to how we move forward and bring the culprits to justice.'

All eyes fastened on to the tall stranger, who now stepped forward.

Brick had been giving a lot of thought to the uninvited responsibility that had been heaped on to his shoulders. The expectant looks from the assembled ranchers made him nervous. He was a loner, unused to leading men into dangerous situations.

Outside, a dog barked. Hens squawked. A horse whinnied.

But the hopeful eyes rested on Brick Shaftoe.

He sucked in a lungful of air. Then, jamming the stub of an old cigar between clenched teeth, he scraped a match across his pants and lit up. It was merely a ploy, a delaying tactic to give him time to reflect on what he could tell these hardy ranchers. How could he allay their fears? The very first question to answer was: what was the source of the firearms being supplied to the Indians? Then cutting it off.

Before he had time to open his

mouth a dark shadow blotted out the light beaming in through the open barn door. A huge bear of a man, broad as he was tall, stood there. His hand rested menacingly on the butt of a holstered .45.

But it was not this man-mountain who commanded Brick's attention.

Beside him stood a stooped, rather insignificant-looking individual. Much smaller in stature, the man had a tanned face much lined by sun and wind. He was clearly no hard-bitten roughneck like his bodyguard. But the slight figure was no less imposing for that. Indeed, he had deep-set, piercing eyes that held the younger man in a mesmerizing gaze.

The hooked nose sniffed the air like a vulture, a scavenger selecting its next picking. Brick had the uneasy feeling that this man was regarding him as would a dangerous predator. A ripple of trepidation rustled down his spine.

The seated ranchers turned to follow Brick's riveted stare.

It was Buckweed Jackson who broke the spell.

'What do you want, Williams?' he growled. 'Your kind ain't welcome here.'

Brick was instantly on his guard. So this was the notorious owner of the Rocking Chair, he mused.

A further notion elbowed any other thought aside. Was this turkey aware of the trouble to which his hired hands had been party? Brick fingered the ugly scar around his neck. Judging by the company the diminutive ranch boss kept, Brick could only assume that Chuck Williams was fully cognisant of everything that occurred in his domain. After all, wasn't the guy here now? Muscling in on a supposedly covert meeting.

'Don't speak to Mr Williams like that,' snarled the grizzly minder, taking a step forward.

The predator held out a restraining hand.

'Take it easy, Knuckles.' A loose smile

playing across the gaunt features held no hint of humour. 'We're guests on Mr Jackson's land. He has a right to enquire as to our motives.' A bleak guffaw hissed from the bony mouth. 'Please excuse my associate. Knuckles has my best interests at heart. He just gets a bit too protective sometimes.'

Bareknuckle Patrick Beesley had acquired his lurid nickname on account of a brutal penchant for fist-fighting. The bruiser relished nothing more than needling like-minded toughs into participating in a contest, for money of course. Thus far he was undefeated.

Brick was about to confront the newcomer about his men's heinous actions when Buckweed Jackson took a pace forward. He was not intimidated by the bodyguard's bullying tactics.

'So what are these so called motives?' rasped the Box J rancher.

'Any meeting of the local cattlemen ought to include the owner of the biggest spread in the territory,' Williams replied, pausing to select a large

Havana from a gold case. Like a trained monkey, Beesley immediately snapped a vesta to ignite the expensive cigar. Allowing wisps of blue smoke to dribble from his thin lips, Williams fixed Jackson with snake-eyed disdain. 'Wouldn't you agree . . . Mr Jackson?'

'Just come to the point,' butted in Joe Sackett. 'What is it you really want?'

'Maybe it's to find out why you didn't ask me to the meeting.'

'You know darned well that it's about these Indian raids. And with all the gunhands you have on your payroll, it don't concern you. Brick Shaftoe here' — Sackett jabbed a thumb at his associate — 'is a special investigator for the Indian Agency.'

On hearing this revelation, Williams visibly stiffened.

'You don't say.' He smirked.

Sackett ignored the interruption. 'He's come to Brass Neck to investigate how the Apache have been able to get their hands on guns and ammo to use against us.'

Another rancher called Jefferson Cartwright stood up to offer his view on the matter. He ran the Panhandle, a small operation at the top end of the valley. His input was aimed directly at the maverick rancher.

'Seems mighty convenient that your operation has been unaffected by any of these darned raids. Each one of us here has had stock taken. The unlucky ones have been burnt out and forced to sell at a cut-down price.'

Cartwright thrust his square jaw forward, challenging the Rocking Chair boss to deny the allegations.

Williams was unfazed.

'They were offered a fair price,' he replied, calmly puffing on the cigar. 'It wasn't my fault those turnips had no backbone. Any murdering Apaches try to invade my place and I'll give 'em a dose of lead poisoning.'

A murmur of indignation rippled through the assembled ranchers.

'That's because you can afford to take on a bunch of hired guns for protection,' snapped an irate Joe Sackett. 'Where can small fry like us find the dough for that?'

Williams shrugged. 'That's your problem.'

'Somebody around here has been supplying guns to the Apache.'

Brick had taken a pace towards the arrogant ranch boss and his minder. His voice was low-keyed but menacing in its delivery. He had come to the conclusion that Williams was either unaware of his foreman's underhanded doings, or uncaring. Either way, he deemed it prudent to keep the matter under wraps. 'And I intend to find out who that varmint is and bring him to justice,' he continued undeterred by the glowering face of Bareknuckle Beesley. 'And be assured, Mr Williams, I'll leave no stone unturned, no rat unsnared.' On uttering that biting comment, Brick fixed the rancher with a baleful glare. 'Until the job is done and I gun down the skunk that killed my brother.'

'Is that a threat, mister?' came back

the cutting riposte.

'Take it anyway you want,' replied Brick. 'The innocent will have nothing to fear . . . or to hide.'

Sackett backed up his house-guest's brave, some might say foolhardy, defiance with his own invective.

'You can't railroad us, Williams,' he hollered, injecting the rush with a biting edge. 'Nobody is gonna force me off my land. I'll die first rather than sell out to the likes of you.'

A sneer of annoyance cracked the nonchalant mien of the vulture. His mouth turned down in a warped twist of anger. With the greatest restraint, Chuck Williams forced himself to remain unperturbed. His bodyguard was all for cutting loose there and then. But the rancher stayed his over-eager hand with a sharp command.

'Leave it, Knuckles!' he rasped. 'Our time will come.' Then he jabbed a clawlike finger towards the ringleader of the group. And in a low yet menacing tone he hissed, 'You oughta be careful what you wish for, Sackett.' The ensuing pause added potency to the predator's closing ultimatum. 'Cos it might well come true.'

And with that last retort, the strutting rancher swung on his heel and stomped away, followed by the lumbering hulk of the bodyguard.

A palpable sigh of relief issued from the gathered ranchers. That was one interloper they were more than glad to see the back of. But they had been left with no illusions as to the land-grabbing ambitions of the Rocking Chair boss. Williams was prepared to go to any lengths to secure his goals.

The main question that troubled Brick Shaftoe's cogitations was whether the grasping toad was mixed up in the Apache raids, and in consequence, his brother's premature demise. It was looking increasingly probable.

And why was he so eager to acquire all this land? There was clearly more to this than met the eye.

Brick also knew that in digging out

the truth he could expect no help from the marshal of Brass Neck. That marrow-munching jasper left his responsibilities at the town limits. And the nearest seat for territorial law enforcement lay seven days ride to the north, at Silver City.

Special Agent Brick Shaftoe was on his own.

8

Guns in the afternoon

It was around noon of the following day.

Brick was idly leaning against the heavy post supporting the veranda that overshadowed the front of the Bar S ranch house. He rolled a quirley and surveyed the landscape stretching away into the distance. It was an idyllic scene. He could well imagine that his brother would have been mighty content to settle down here with the girl of his dreams.

A smile hovered on his face as he perceived young Wink Montoya wrestling with a feisty calf over in the corral. The newborn was clearly winning the contest causing the young man to utter some uncharacteristic language.

Wink was shaking his arms about. He

seemed to have lost his temper. Not like the boy at all, Brick surmised. He was usually so calm and composed. Brick shook his head, recognizing that help was needed.

'Now then, boy,' he muttered to himself. 'That ain't no way to get the job done.' Levering himself off the wooden prop, he ground out the half-smoked quirley and made to head off in the direction of the trial of strength.

Had he been a second later in making that fateful decision, Brick Shaftoe would have found himself pinned to the heavy brace by an Apache arrow. As it was, his Stetson bore the brunt of the well-placed shaft which quivered and hummed in the static air no more than two inches from his bulky torso.

So that was why the boy was hollering like a demented banshee. In the flick of a rattler's tongue Brick had dived for cover behind the nearby water trough. The Colt Frontier jumped into his right hand. Keen eyes panned the open ground close to the ranch buildings.

A flicker of movement over behind a clump of wilting cottonwoods told him where the bushwhackers were concealed. Without further thought, he loosed off three shots while yelling for the youngster to join him.

'Over here, Wink!' Alarm and fear for the boy's safety lent an intense urgency to the strident command. 'And keep your head down!'

Then he emptied the shooter into the emerging band of Indians. None of the bullets found its mark. But the threat of an early visit to the happy hunting grounds stayed the full-blown charge sufficiently for the pair to scramble back into the safety of the sturdy log house.

'What in tarnation is all the shootin' about?' demanded a startled Joe Sackett, who had been repairing a frayed saddle horn.

More arrows thudding into the

recently slammed door gave him some inkling that danger was close by. One sang through an open window to bury itself in the wall above his head. Its arrival effectively answered his question. And if that wasn't enough, a whooping and a hollering of frenzied Apaches outside convinced the cabin's occupants that they were under attack.

'You take that window, gal,' Sackett shouted at his daughter. Then to Wink he snapped, 'And you take that one on the far side. Me and Brick will cover the front.'

Discarding the saddle, the rancher lunged for a Spencer carbine propped above the fireplace. He grabbed a box of cartridges from the dresser before hustling across to the open window, which he immediately slammed shut. Small holes in the thick shutter had been cut out for just such an eventuality. All the other windows were similarly provided.

Martha Sackett was equally at home with a skillet or needle and thread, as well as the Ballard breach-loader that she now snatched from its home in the far corner of the room. Checking that the gun had a load up the spout, she hurried across to the position indicated by her father.

The small room slowly filled with black powder smoke as the defenders retaliated with vigour. An acrid stench of burnt cordite stung their nostrils and made their eyes water. And it was hot as hell on a Saturday night.

Three Indians lay dead in the yard outside the cabin. The others, recognizing that this would be no easy task, had retreated to the cover afforded by the small copse.

From the brief glimpses he'd had Brick estimated that there must be around thirty Apaches still out there. The white folks were safe for the time being. But Brick was under no illusions that the attackers would give up the fight. Nor would any quarter be given.

Apaches were doggedly brave warriors. But at least their arsenal was limited. They appeared to have only a handful of old rifles: Springfields and Leman flintlocks. But those weapons were no use on horseback. Consequently, many Indians still favoured the age-old use of bow and arrow.

A delivery of fast-action repeaters would be more than welcome to the Apache chief. And Manganellis would be willing to pay in gold to get his hands on them. Such a formidable addition to his firepower would appreciably improve the ability of the Apache raiders to conquer any foe.

Whoever was behind the gun-running had a lot to answer for.

The next two hours witnessed a desultory firing from the concealed Indians who kept the defenders on their toes. But they didn't have things all their own way.

'Yee haar!' shrieked a jubilant Wink Montoya. 'Got me another of those smelly *motetas*. That make two now.'

But neither side was getting the upper hand. Sackett and his *compadres* were effectively pinned down in the cabin with nowhere to go. The Indians had tried to rush them on a couple of occasions, with the loss of two braves each time. But they had plenty more to call on.

Stalemate. Something had to give.

Brick was aware that many Indians were loath to continue a conflict after dark. Spiritual retreat of the sun god was judged to weaken their ability to overcome the enemy. So unless they made a move soon, the defenders could probably rest easy until dawn heralded a renewed and much more full-blooded endeavour. There was still around five hours of daylight remaining.

Much could still happen before nightfall.

Manganellis had clearly been reading Brick Shaftoe's mind and had arrived at the same conclusion.

Nothing had happened for a half-hour. Not a single shot was fired, nor an arrow loosed. Brick wrinkled his brow in thought. What were the scheming dogs up to? The Apache chief was no mulehead. A more intelligent Indian he had yet to encounter. He was hatching some nefarious plan to smoke them out.

How those thoughts were to come back and haunt him.

Five minutes later Joe Sackett's bulbous snout twitched. Smoke from the guns had dispersed. But this was a different odour.

It was the ever perceptive Wink Montoya who provided the solution to his bafflement.

'*Humo! Humo! Y Incendio!*'

The boy's windmilling arms pointed skywards. The others followed his staring eyes.

Smoke was filtering through the sod roof. Already, tongues of orange flame were licking at the heavy support beams. Crackling and popping like witless chickens, the burning of the tinder-dry vegetation spread rapidly — a rampant plague consuming all in its path. It was only a matter of time before the whole lot went up.

Martha was the first to snap out of the hypnotic inertia that shocked terror induces. She snatched up the bucket of water beside the fireplace and tossed it at the sizzling flames. It was an act precipitated by pure desperation and had little effect on the burgeoning conflagration.

Her next thought was to dash outside to refill the bucket.

It was a calamitous decision. Had panic not gripped her soul, Martha Sackett might well have hesitated.

'Don't go out there!' yelled her father.

But it was too late. A well-placed lead ball from an ancient Leman struck her in the chest.

Joe screamed.

'Go out and drag her back in here while I cover you.' Brick's brittle charge to Joe Sackett was accompanied by a furious volley from his Winchester at the hidden enemy.

But Sackett was in shock. He stood

anchored to the spot, unhearing, unable to respond to Brick's urgent directive.

'Get out there now, Joe!' howled Brick, injecting a acid bite into the words. 'Otherwise Martha will die for sure.'

The robust warning was enough to precipitate the distraught rancher into action.

'Yeah! Yeah! I'm on to it,' he croaked, ducking low as he hustled out of the door and over to the prostrate form of his daughter.

Brick emptied the rest of the rifle's magazine at the hovering foe. A single cry on the far side of the corral brought a smile to his grim features. The volley delayed a full-blown charge by the Indians. A brief respite only, but sufficient to enable the rancher to drag his stricken daughter back into the dubious safety of the cabin.

But for how long?

The old rancher had managed to rescue his daughter without any further injury to himself or the girl. But he was close to tears. His hunched frame slumped down beside the still body of his only child. All around them thickening smoke crept over the room. A burning clump of dried grass fell from the roof.

Sparks fizzed and sizzled on the woollen floor-mat and immediately caught fire. Brick stamped out the spreading flames. Outside, the strident yelps of triumph from the gathering Apache told him that they were ready to make their final play.

'She still alive,' shouted Wink. It was only a slight movement of the head that had attracted the boy's attention. But it was enough to bring a sigh of relief to the defenders. Though only for an instant.

'We ain't got time for no mooning over what's happened,' Brick rapped. Roughly he shook the crazed father's bent form. 'If'n we don't leave now, it's curtains for us all.'

'We can use the wagon out back,' suggested a suddenly rejuvenated Joe

Sackett. 'At least it will give us some breathing space.'

'You help Joe while I keep these varmints busy,' Brick said to Wink. 'I'll catch you up soon as I can.'

'Do not be too long, Señor Brick,' advised the boy jabbing a thumb towards the crackling inferno overhead.

Even now, the roof was threatening imminent collapse.

The Indian agent returned Wink's anxious gaze with a brisk nod.

'Be with you afore you know it,' he promised. 'Now get after that wagon. I'm counting on you to keep them out of harm's way.'

He untied the bandanna from around his neck and briskly stroked away the thick film of dirt and sweat coating his stubbled cheeks and forehead. A quick drink from the canteen followed. Now he was ready for anything Manganellis could throw at him.

At least that was the impression he had hoped to impress on the boy.

In truth, his legs were shaking. A

band of screaming Apaches charging down on you is apt to make the stoutest of hearts quake. And Brick's pounding ticker was no exception. But he knew that it was up to him to give Joe Sackett a head start. The chance to reach Buckweed Jackson's ranch unscathed. It was a larger spread than the Bar S, and Jackson employed three ranch hands.

Manganellis would need to think twice about attacking such a place with his current array of weaponry. But if the Indian warrior got his hands on repeating rifles, it would surely imbue him with the conviction that he was invincible, and that victory would be assured.

A muted crack of the whip sounded from behind the ranch house and Brick knew that the wagon and its occupants were on the move. This was confirmed by a renewed outburst of hollering from the attackers. They veered left of the cabin, assuming that all the occupants had fled.

It came as something of surprise when the leading rider threw up his arms and tumbled from his horse. Brick's next aim was to take Manganellis out of the fracas. Removing their leader would throw the rest of band into disarray. And the imposing figure was easy to spot.

Tall and statuesque, he sported an intricately woven war bonnet prepared by the tribal medicine man. The headgear was intended to give him immunity from bullets. It had worked perfectly so far. Following each charge at the enemy, Manganellis had emerged totally unscathed.

But his luck had to run out at some point. And that moment had arrived.

Taking careful aim, Brick squeezed the trigger. He had the satisfaction of witnessing the mighty warrior chieftain crashing to the ground. But instantly, he was on his feet and weaving back to the safety of the cottonwood grove.

Brick cursed aloud. He could have sworn the guy was a goner.

Manganellis had received only a glancing blow. The famed war bonnet appeared to be still exercising its magical powers upon the wearer. But at least the rest of tribe had been halted in their tracks.

Without further ado, Brick left the cabin and scooted round the back where his own horse was waiting. Shadow whinnied appreciatively on seeing her master: a more hearty greeting than was customary.

But the rider was given no opportunity to mount up.

A heavy weight struck him solidly in the middle of the back. The sudden jolt sent him sprawling on the ground. But he was lucky. Had the deadly stone-headed war club connected properly, it would have smashed his head in. Brick was extremely fortunate that the faithful cayuse had sensed the danger and nudged her master out of the line of attack. Even so, the force of the blow had stunned him.

The blood-curdling death chant that

now pierced the stricken man's torpid brain was enough to inform him that the grim reaper was close at hand. Unable to move a muscle, Brick was at the mercy of his enemy.

A shadow blocked out the sun. Brick closed his eyes, waiting for Death to leave his calling card.

Time stood still. Then the sudden ripple of gunfire chocked off the braying chant. A body thudded into the ground next to him. It was that of a fully painted-up Apache brave.

'You lucky fellow, Brick Shaftoe. No can leave partner alone. Or good self will come to harm.'

The lilting Mexican cadence was music to his ears.

Already the boy was heaving him to his feet. Both knew they had no time to waste if they were to continue thwarting the Scythe Man. Manganellis also appeared to have recovered. Seeing their chief rise from the dead had given the Indians renewed vigour. They were massing for a final assault. And this time Brick was sure they would not be frustrated in their blood lust.

Human instinct for survival now kicked in.

Brick somehow found the strength to mount his horse. The animal needed no encouragement to leave the lethal killing ground. Clouds of dust rose into the air as hoofs dug deep. And soon both partners were galloping headlong after the ranch wagon.

Only when they were out of the enclosed confines of Bar S land and into more open country did Brick check whether the Apache were still in pursuit.

A sigh of relief hissed from between clenched teeth.

Manganellis must have been feeling as rough as Brick Shaftoe and decided to withdraw from the conflict. Their back trail was clear.

'You and me saving each other's hide is becoming a habit.' Brick grinned at the beaming youngster as he held out a hand. 'Partner.'

9

Know your enemy

Though exhausted following the Indian raid, Brick had insisted on riding immediately to Brass Neck in order to secure the urgent medical attention needed for Martha Sackett. Only the settling influence of Maisy Jackson had made him see sense. Urging restraint, she had gently persuaded the impatient man that much-needed rest and sustenance would work wonders. He had reluctantly agreed, and then promptly fallen asleep in a rocking-chair.

Only after the evening meal was he at last allowed to make the three-hour trip from the Box J to Brass Neck.

Brick had reached the Sisters of Mercy hospital in Brass Neck around midnight. Consuela knew at a glance that the dusty apparition was badly in need of sleep. With pressing insistence she propelled him upstairs to his room. He was asleep even before his head hit the pillow.

They had set off from Brass Neck at first light and Brick had enjoyed every second of the journey. It ought to have been a sombre trip. But nothing short of a bullet in the guts was going to spoil the young man's harmonious rapport with the woman of his dreams. And judging by the smile that illuminated her smoothly dark features, Consuela had been equally smitten.

Mid-morning found the two riders on Box J land. But it was another half-hour before the cluster of ranch buildings hove into view. As they passed beneath a gateway sporting the ranch brand emblazoned on to the bleached head of a steer, their arrival jolted them back to the bleak reality of their situation.

'I hope we are in time to help poor Martha,' voiced the concerned nurse. 'With her fiancé dead, and now the ranch burnt down, she will need all the support we can give her.'

Brick could only intone a murmur of agreement.

But their fervent prayers were in vain. Martha Sackett had passed away during the night.

'She regained consciousness,' sobbed a distraught Maisy Jackson, dabbing her eyes. 'But it was only for a few minutes. Then she . . . '

But the recollection was too much for the older woman.

She sank into a chair, the comforting arm of her husband trying ineffectually to heal the pain. The Sacketts were their nearest neighbours. And Maisy had become a surrogate mother to the young girl following the untimely death of her own mother from the fever.

'Where's Joe?'

Only now did Brick realize that the Bar S owner was missing, along with the Mexican boy.

'He took Martha back to the ranch. Or what's left of it,' said Buckweed.

'Said he was gonna lay the poor girl next to her mother,' interjected Maisy Jackson. 'Consuela's brother went along to help out with the burial.'

'Old Joe was struggling to get his head round what has happened,' sighed the Box J rancher. Bent shoulders dropped resignedly. 'I tried to get him to stay here. But he's a stubborn old cuss. All fired-up, he was. Angrier than a wounded grizzly. Gave me the impression he was gonna take on the whole Apache nation.'

'I'd better get over there,' announced Brick.

'And I am coming with you,' declared Consuela.

'No way! It's too dangerous,' countered Brick. He was more than a touch anxious for the girl's safety. 'You return to Brass Neck and — '

'No buts!' exclaimed the girl adamantly. 'Pepe is over there. The Indians could return at any time. What kind of a sister would I be to let my only kin face them alone?'

136

'But I will be there with Joe Sackett,' stressed Brick.

'Don't leave me out of this shindig,' interrupted Buckweed Jackson displaying an ardent resolve.

Consuela remained tight-lipped, her darkly hypnotic eyes flashing and defiant. With slow deliberation she raised her proud head, black tresses swishing in majestic disdain. It was an emphatic challenge for any man, even Brick Shaftoe, to deny her an equal hearing.

'And besides,' she asserted fervently, 'Consuela Montoya de Santiago is the best rifle shot in Sonora. Can either of you deny that an extra gun will not come in very handy?'

Hands placed provocatively on her swaying hips, the Mexican girl stood her ground.

Both men knew when they had met their match.

Brick gave a helpless shrug. He was deeply unsettled, but equally proud.

Maisy Jackson likewise accepted her

husband's decision to support their stricken neighbour. It was an unwritten law of the frontier. And they would have expected no less had the boot been assigned to the other foot.

'I will have some vittles ready within the half-hour,' she announced, rising purposefully to her feet. 'Who knows when you will get the opportunity for a decent meal?'

The distress occasioned by recent events was now consigned to a storeroom in the back of her mind. There would be more than enough time for private grief when she was alone.

★　★　★

The sun was settling down towards the western horizon when the three riders eventually drew up outside the smouldering embers of what had once been a small yet thriving ranch. Tendrils of white smoke filtered from between the blackened husk of the charred beams.

In the open ground of the corral dark

stains in the sand pointed to where the bodies of dead Indians had once been. But now they had been removed for a proper dispatch to the happy hunting grounds in time-honoured fashion.

Indians consider this to be a vital element of their journey into the afterlife. To be denied that privilege means that the soul is left in limbo, forced to wander aimlessly in an obscure world of unbelonging and heartache.

Over on the far side of the corral, in the shade of a large cottonwood, two graves could be clearly seen. One of recent origin must be that of Martha Sackett. Wink was busy tidying up the small plot. But of the rancher himself there was no sign.

So had he already left to pursue his blinkered course of vengeance? It was out of character for him to have left the Mexican boy alone.

Brick's musing was abruptly cut short by a spine-tingling howl of agony. It emanated from behind an outhouse on the far side of the corral, one that had escaped the conflagration. A plume of dark woodsmoke rose from behind the solitary building.

'What in tarnation is that?' exclaimed a startled Brick Shaftoe.

'It came from over yonder.' Jackson pointed to the stone-built root store.

Another searing scream rent the static air. Somebody was clearly in extreme pain.

'Let's go!' hollered Brick.

Racing across the open stretch of ground, the new arrivals shot round the corner of the building to witness a blood-curdling scenario.

Joe Sackett had clearly not vacated his ruined premises.

In his right hand was a branding-iron. The tip displaying the ranch logo of a barred S glowed bright orange. With the other he had a firm grip on the long hair of an Apache brave. The sickly odour of burnt flesh stung their nostrils, proving that the iron had already been applied.

The Indian was little more than a boy and this had likely been his first raid. And it looked all set to be his last. Brick quickly surmised that he must have been overlooked by the rest of the tribe when they came back to retrieve the bodies of their fallen comrades. Blood dripping from a scalp wound also indicated that the Indian was already badly wounded before Sackett got to work on him.

'Spill the beans, you scurvy dog,' bellowed the incensed rancher, roughly shaking the dying Indian. Standing over the helpless youngster, he looked ready to deliver the *coup de grâce*. 'Who's been sellin' you them guns?'

Consuela and Buckweed Jackson were both stunned into immobility. The stomach-churning brutality of the interrogation was more than either had ever encountered before.

Only Brick was unaffected by such barbarity. The Apache were renowned for their own brand of physical cruelty towards enemies. And the Indian agent had witnessed the bloodthirsty torments perpetrated on white captives. He had no sympathy for the young brave.

But this was not the way to secure much-needed information from a newly accredited brave. Warrior tribes were disciplined to endure pain from an early age and would choose to die rather than submit to the shame of capitulation. Only true fighters could enter the gates of Heaven.

Two quick strides saw Brick booting the lethal branding-iron aside.

Sackett was taken by surprise.

'What the hell!' he stormed, swinging on his heel to face this new threat. On seeing who had prevented what he considered due vengeance for his daughter's killing, the incensed rancher growled, 'Why d'yuh do that? You some kinda Indian-lover, Shaftoe? This bastard was about to give me the answers to where them guns are comin' from.'

'And that ain't the way to go about it,' replied Brick forcefully. 'These guys'll gladly hit the high trail rather than lose face by giving in to a white man.'

'And you'd know about that, I suppose.' Sackett's retort was acerbic.

'Darned right I do. I'm an Indian agent. It's my business to know.'

'So what's your angle, mister?' sneered the big rancher. His fists were balled and he looked all set to attack the younger man. 'Invite him to the next barn dance if'n he plays ball?'

Brick ignored the taunt. 'There are other ways, Joe,' he said, keeping his voice low and even. 'This kid would rather die than give in to bullying tactics from a white man. The Apache are a highly superstitious people. They place a heap of faith in the gods. Judging by those injuries, he likely knows he's headed in that direction.' Brick's square chin jutted forward to emphasize the next point. 'I can ensure he makes it into the fold to commune with his forebears in peace and harmony. And to achieve that he'll do anything.'

'Including giving up the information we need, I suppose?'

'You got it in one, Joe,' Brick confirmed.

Sackett's twisted grimace indicated what he thought of such idealistic eyewash.

But it was Wink Montoya who defused the tense stand-off. He rushed to intervene and stood between the twitchy duo.

'Señor Sackett, is it not true that you want revenge for your daughter's death?'

'Sure,' grunted the rancher. 'So what?'

'And wouldn't you be willing to try any means to learn who is behind all these attacks?'

Sackett gave a perfunctory nod of irritation.

'Get to the point, kid,' he snapped.

'Then what have you to lose by allowing Señor Brick to try his way?' The Mexican boy's eye twitched alarmingly. Then he offered the rancher a wry smile. 'He does, after all, have

144

much experience in dealing with these *valientes*.' Hands raised skywards indicated that it was the most sensible option, but that the final decision was now in the hands of the rancher.

Joe Sackett stood his ground. He was torn between the logic of his compadres and an inborn desire for brutal retaliation for his loss.

Consuela now stepped up in support of this new option.

'My brother speaks good sense, *señor*,' she purred laying her hands on Wink's curly mop of black hair. 'There is much wisdom on these young shoulders.'

The soothing lilt helped to calm the ruffled feelings of the fiery cowman. He hesitated for another ten seconds before his shoulders slumped. Turning to hide the tears welling up his old eyes, he sat down on a barrel.

'Have it your own way then,' he muttered. 'I only hope that it works.'

Brick slapped the rancher on the back.

'Don't you fret none.' He smiled, while releasing a sigh of relief. 'My way is gonna work. I guarantee it.'

Consuela then ushered the rancher over to where they had tethered the horses and offered him some much-appreciated ham tortillas and apple pie.

'I'll make the coffee,' offered Wink.

'I could sure use some,' replied the rancher matching the boy's disarming manner with a subdued grin of accord.

Joe was feeling rather shamefaced about his loss of control regarding the incident. He made a subdued attempt to voice an apology, explaining away the red mist as a reaction to the recent attacks and the loss of his daughter.

'It ain't like me at all,' he mumbled, slurping down a mouthful of hot coffee. 'The old fella down below musta got to diggin' at my guts. Turned my head. And when that Indian stumbled into the open . . . ' He shook his head at the recollection. 'Well . . . I just saw red. All the anger and frustration came bustin' out in one fell swoop.'

'It OK now, *señor*,' murmured Consuela, patting his bent shoulders. 'I can understand how you feel. Nobody should have to lose a loved one like that.'

The mollifying words helped assuage the old rancher's conscience. He nodded his thanks to the girl.

It was another half-hour before Brick rejoined them. There was a grim set to his chiselled features.

'Did you learn anything?' enquired the ever-eager Wink Montoya.

Brick did not reply at first. His hooded eyes were fixed on the distant horizon. As if in a dream, he rolled a quirley and lit up. The effect of the smoke drawn deep into his lungs appeared to bring him back to reality.

'Sure did,' came the flat response. 'And it don't make for easy listening.' He took another long drag on the smokepole before telling them.

10

A Spirited Departure

Horse Tail was well down the path of no return when Brick gently propped him up against the root-cellar wall. He dribbled some water down the young brave's throat before flatly informing him that the great spirit had come to claim his dues. With injuries such as he had suffered, there was no way back. And he should prepare himself to enter the afterlife.

'You can't do that without my help,' Brick stressed, emphasizing his suggestion that such assistance came at a price. He paused to let this idea register in the kid's fevered brain. 'We need to know from where the Apache are getting their stock of firesticks.'

Though hovering on the brink, the proud Apache affected a doughty resolve. And he still managed to convey his disdain for the white man's request by remaining tight-lipped. Arrogantly he turned his blood-caked head away.

'Have it your own way, kid.' Brick's shoulders lifted in a meaningful shrug of indifference. He stood up and made to leave the dying Indian. 'I take it you ain't concerned about receiving a proper send-off then? Rather get stuck in the netherworld, would you?' Another shrug was accompanied by a comment laced with phlegmatic disinterest. 'Don't matter none to me if'n your soul stays in limboland, forever condemned to roam the wretched prairies of eternal damnation. Still, if that's what you want.'

He hitched up his gunbelt, set his hat straight and made ready to depart.

'Wait.'

The guttural croak was music to Brick's ears. His whole body tensed. Had the ploy worked? He forced himself to continue walking away.

Again: 'Wait! Wait!'

Brick paused in mid-stride.

'Horse Tail want . . . assurance from white eyes . . . that proper rites will be performed . . . once Earth life finished.' The words emerged in a series of staccato bursts, each phrase painfully dredged from deep within, and each weaker than the last.

The Indian agent knew that the Apache youth did not have much longer to live. Still he held back, forcing himself to remain calmly stoic. The boy would expect nothing less.

Then, slowly, and with composed deliberation, he swung on his heel, laying a cool eye on to the stricken brave. Hoarse breath rasping harshly in his throat told the white man that Horse Tail was in great pain.

'You have my word,' he whispered, ensuring that the utterance lacked any form of emotive connotation. He slapped his chest firmly. 'Brickhill Shaftoe is an honest Indian agent who knows the Apache people to be a proudly bold and determined race. I respect their beliefs, and will ensure that Horse Tail is accorded the full honours deserving of one who has fallen in battle.'

The Indian forced a smile and nodded.

'Then draw close and listen, white man,' he rasped. 'Ask what you will. But make haste, for there is not much time left for me on this Earth.'

★ ★ ★

'Come on, fella,' pressed Joe Sackett who had regained much of his old *joie de vivre*. 'So what did you find out from that red devil?'

Many were the good points that Buckweed Jackson could have extolled about his old buddy, but patience was most definitely not one of them.

'Let the guy tell us in his own good time, Joe,' he counselled.

'Joe's right,' said Brick. 'We ain't got much time if what Horse Tail revealed is on the level. And I'm darned sure it is.'

He then proceeded to elaborate on the vital information that the Indian had surrendered in exchange for a harmonious passage into the afterlife.

It appeared that a wagon containing new repeaters was being moved across the border in the next few days. Horse Tail was unsure of the exact time, but was certain that delivery was imminent. Now came the important bit. It was Chuck Williams and his bunch of hired gunslicks who were behind the illegal transaction.

'I knew that guy wasn't on the level,' railed Sackett. His pockmarked kisser coloured to a russet hue as wild fury tore at the big guy's innards. 'The scheming rat must have some hidden motive, wanting to drive us all off this land.'

'Did the Indian have any notion about that?' enquired Jackson.

Brick shook his head. 'All the Apache are concerned about is getting even with those they reckon are stealing their tribal lands. And I can't rightly blame them for that. But the Indian Agency has been set up to keep the peace and help the tribes settle on to the alloted reservations. That's part of my job.' His eyes narrowed, his square jaw was set firm. A hard look of granite-edged resolve accompanied his final declaration.

'Now that it's been made clear that the Rocking Chair is responsible for Tom's death, I aim to see it through to the end and bring those critters to justice.' He paused to draw breath. 'Or die trying.'

Consuela ran over and took both his hands in hers. Lines of worry marred the girl's aquiline profile.

'You not tackle these devils alone,' she protested vehemently. 'You now *mi enamorado*. We do this thing together, *sí?*'

A startled look passed over the Indian agent's face. Her ardent gaze, warm and inviting, was totally unexpected. It filled him with a passionate yearning. Yet he hesitated, torn between a boundless love and duty.

Deep within his being, Brick knew that the one could not come to fruition without a satisfactory conclusion to the other. So, with great reluctance, he forced aside an overwhelming desire to take this Angel of Mercy into his arms. Much as he welcomed the girl's presumptuous assertion, this was not the moment to declare any such sentiments.

'S-sure thing, Consuela,' he stammered. 'But let's just take one step at a time, eh?'

Joe Sackett coughed.

'We'd best be gathering up the rest of the boys,' he commented. 'If'n we're to stand any chance of staving off a bloodbath, then we need more firepower. Williams ain't gonna surrender them guns without a fight.' The rancher was already striding across to his horse.

'There's no time for that,' asserted Brick. 'Them guns could be coming through the San Luis pass at this very moment. Rounding up a sizeable band will take too long.'

'So what are you suggestin'?' demanded Sackett. 'That we take 'em by ourselves? That's mighty risky, don't you think?'

Brick thought for a moment.

'Buckweed here is chairman of the Cattlemen's Association. He could call on the support of the smaller spreads and meet us as soon as possible at the pass.' Addressing Jackson, he added, 'If we get there first, surprise will be on our side and we could hold them off for a spell until you arrive.'

'It is a narrow ravine,' interjected young Montoya, anxious not to be left out of the proceedings. 'I come through there recently. Three guns easily stop wagon. But need to set off now. Long and dangerous ride.' He threw a poignant glance towards Brick. The agent nodded his understanding.

'Then let's be hittin' the trail,' replied Sackett, mounting up. He was chafing at the bit, anxious to be on the move.

Brick raised a hand to stop him.

155

'There's one thing that needs our attention afore we strike out,' he said, holding the big man's twitchy regard.

'And what's that?'

'Horse Tail needs to be given a proper funeral.'

The Bar S owner scoffed. 'Far as I'm concerned, every good Indian is a dead'un.' He dragged his horse around ready to spur off.

Brick grabbed a hold of the bridle, holding the large bay mare steady.

'This act is something that has to be done,' he stressed, holding the big man's gaze.

His words were spoken in a quiet yet resolute manner. He sympathized with the rancher's attitude concerning Apache tradition and heritage. But Brick Shaftoe was nothing if not a man of his word.

'I made a promise. The kid handed over the particulars we were after. It's only right and proper that I keep my end of the bargain.' He laid a conciliatory hand on the rancher's arm.

'A man of your stature, admired and respected as being just and fair-minded throughout the territory, would expect nothing less of a buddy.' At this point, Brick's stern countenance softened as he offered up the hint of a smile to the granite-faced frontiersman. 'Would he, Joe?' Then, on a lighter note, he added, 'Won't take but an hour at the most. So what d'yuh say?'

The others waited. It was Sackett's decision. He had lost the most in this fracas. And Buckweed Jackson for one, would respect his friend's decision, whatever that might be.

The Bar S rancher's hard exterior crumpled. This was the second time his stubborn streak had been tamed by this dynamic Indian agent.

'Seems like I'm forever bein' humbled by you, son,' he muttered slowly, infusing the remark with a measure of unease as he dismounted. 'You've got yourself a deal. But don't be makin' a habit of it. My view of these red devils ain't changed a jot.'

Brick nodded his agreement. He had no wish to damage the old guy's standing among the others.

Quickly they headed back towards the root-cellar. Only Joe Sackett remained with the horses. Pride prevented him from participating in what he considered a heathen ritual.

Within a half-hour they had laid a platform of charred timbers between the raised branches of two adjoining cottonwoods. With some degree of respect, Brick lifted the Apache youth, carried him over to the funeral site and gently laid him on the boards. After folding the dead boy's arms across his chest he stood back.

The others ranged in behind as he mumbled a few suitable mantras. Words such as 'spirits' and 'afterlife' featured heavily. Spiralling columns of ochre sand blew around the twin cotton-woods, the low soughing of the wind lending an eerie feel to the proceedings.

The melancholy funereal platform was above shoulder level, just high enough to prevent marauding coyotes and other such predators from despoiling the corpse.

The cadaver would lie, undefiled, thus enabling the soul to rise freely into the heavens where it would be welcomed into the spirit world.

Sackett's morbid curiosity had got the better of him. He had wandered across to watch the ceremony, but was now itching to get started.

'You folks ready?' he queried, checking the load of his hogleg for the fourth time in the last hour. To his credit, the rancher was not one to bear a grudge or harbour misgivings. While the others had been preparing the dispatch of Horse Tail to the happy hunting grounds, he had gotten in the supplies that would be needed for a trek down to the San Luis pass.

By the time that Brick announced their departure, everything was in order.

'Much obliged for your help, Joe,' he said. 'It's greatly appreciated.' He accepted the big man's curt nod with a tight smile, knowing that everything was now right between them.

By late afternoon they were heading south into the badlands of the Hidalgo Pyramids. Already the westering sun was dipping towards the distant peaks. Brick was well aware of the bleak nature of this austere wilderness and made sure that extra water skins were carried on the packmule.

It was a three-day ride. So there was no room for any more delays if they were to catch the gun-runners on the hop.

11

Missed Opportunity

It was late morning of the third day when the trio of riders eventually reached the San Luis pass.

Tiers of orange-red sandstone loomed up on either side of the narrowing split. Cholla cactus flourished amidst the profusion of Palo Verde trees adding a touch of gold and green to the desolate landscape. Tamarisk and catclaw joined the ubiquitous saltbush along the dried-up river bed that faded into the wild terrain as they entered the confines of the pass. A horny gila monster scuttled beneath a rock while half a dozen cactus wrens perched on a handy saguaro branch, eyeing the passing intruders.

There were other ways through the Hidalgo Pyramids, but this was the only viable route for a heavily laden wagon.

Brick called a halt before they reached the narrow gap.

'Check your weapons,' he ordered. 'We don't want them varmints to surprise us. Stay here while I go ahead and scout the lie of the land.'

Sackett voiced an objection.

'I don't think we should split up,' he protested.

But Brick's logic won him over.

'They could already have spotted us and be lying in wait,' he argued. 'Seems foolish for all of us to just mosey on up there right into an ambush. If'n they get me, at least you have the chance to get out alive.'

'Good figurin',' agreed the rancher. 'But I still don't see why it can't be me what takes the risks.'

'Don't try and fool me that your sight ain't failing, Joe,' replied Brick, trying gently to reveal that he was aware of the rancher's hidden problem. 'I've seen them spectacles you try to keep hidden away. And don't deny that this job needs someone with eagle-eyed vision.'

Sackett's gnarled face reddened. He knew when to accept defeat gracefully.

'OK, mister,' he concurred. 'But you take it careful-like.'

'I intend to for all our sakes.'

A soft look passed between Brick and Consuela.

Then he swung his mount away and nudged it along the narrow deer-run that they had been following.

Thereafter, for the last mile progress was slow and measured. Rifle cocked and ready, Brick's keen gaze nervously scanned the broken terrain for any sign of the gunrunners. Nothing moved amidst the harsh topography.

A half-hour later he returned.

A woebegone shake of the head informed the others that something was wrong.

'We're too late.' The doleful announcement brought a startled question from Joe Sackett.

'What's the matter?' he asked brusquely.

'The wagon has already come through the pass.'

'How d'yuh know that?'

'There was only one set of wagon-wheel ruts,' shot back the edgy Indian agent. Sackett's truculent manner was starting to irritate him. 'And they were new. Not more than six or seven hours old.'

'Could have been some other dudes totin' gear,' contended Sackett.

'No way!' snapped a waspish Brick. 'This route is not on the main trails over the border. The only critters likely to use it are those who are on the dodge, or shipping in illicit goods.'

'Like guns,' cut in Wink Montoya in support of his partner.

'You got it, Wink.'

'So what can we do now?' grumbled Sackett.

'We'll have to follow the tracks and hope the guns haven't been passed on to the Indians before we catch up.'

'Then we ain't got a moment to lose,'

said the anxious rancher, spurring off up the trail.

* * *

After three hours of dogging the twin lines snaking off into the distance there was still no sign of the wagon and its double-dealing guardians.

Brick called a halt.

He removed a sweat-stained hat, wetted his bandanna and fastened it around his neck. A single mouthful of the carefully conserved water followed. There was no knowing when the next chance to fill their depleted canteens would present itself.

His probing eyes surveyed the bleak terrain.

'Can you see anything?' asked a frustrated Joe Sackett, squinting through the wire-rimmed eye-glasses. The affliction didn't sit well on the old dude's shoulders. 'Surely we ought to have caught 'em up by now?'

'Nary a flicker.' The Indian agent

suppressed a murmur of irritation. 'They must be making good time. Probably got a team of four hauling that wagon,' he observed laconically.

At that moment something shot underneath Consuela's paint mare, causing the animal to rear up in fright.

'It all right, *mi hermana*,' remarked her brother with a laugh. 'Only a cheeky roadrunner scared by our noise.'

'Them fellas can burn up the ground at a tidy pace when they've a mind,' added Sackett, joining in the hilarity as the strange creature darted up the trail before disappearing under a clump of prickly pear. It helped to lighten the tense mood.

Picking up the pace to a gentle canter, they set off again.

Half an hour later the clear trail suddenly terminated at a large slab of flat rock.

Brick organized a search of the immediate vicinity to determine which direction the wagon had taken. Already a stiff wind was building, which threatened to fill in the clearly defined wagon ruts. Returning after a brief foray, the others all shook their heads when questioned.

'So which way from here?'

As expected, it was Sackett who asked the obvious question.

'The trail runs straight and true right up to this rocky shelf,' Brick stated, leaning forward in the saddle. 'I reckon we should continue due north and hope to pick it up on the far side.' His pragmatic nature put aside any thoughts of failure. 'Keep your eyes peeled for signs of the wagon ruts when we cross any sandy bits.'

The pace slowed to that of a desert tortoise.

Heads were bent low over the necks of the mounts. Probing eyes avidly perused the rough desert carpet when bare rock surrended to a more broken landscape. They rode in line, approximately fifteen feet separating each horse. That way a much wider area could be covered.

And it worked.

An hour later, Wink emitted a high-pitched yelp of delight in his own tongue. He was on the end of the line and had strayed further to the left, circling behind the protrusion of a solitary organ-pipe cactus.

'Over here, I have found it!'

'Good on yuh, kid,' praised Sackett, slapping the boy on the back. Brick surveyed the direction in which the wagon ruts were pointing.

'Looks like they're heading up into those rocks,' he surmised, pointing a gloved hand towards the line of broken rocks jutting from the desert plain.

'How in tarnation can anyone get a pesky wagon up there?' moaned Sackett, scratching his thinning pate in bewilderment.

'There must be a way,' replied Brick. 'It can't just have disappeared into thin air. All we can do is keep a close watch for any movement that'll give away their hideout.'

'Easier for one person to go up there,

señores,' voiced Wink. 'And safer. Lone rider not get spotted so easily.'

'Sounds good to me,' agreed Brick. He dragged his rifle out of the saddle boot and jacked in a round. 'Be back afore you know it.'

Wink laid a restraining hand on Brick's arm.

'My turn this time, *compadre*,' he insisted firmly before hurrying on to justify his assertion. 'Are we not partners?'

'Sure but — '

'And partners share everything. No?'

'I guess so.'

'Then it is only fair that Wink Montoya Bavispe de Santiago shoulder his share of responsibility. Face danger with head held high.' Wink's young face was set in stone, his thin frame stiffly upright in the saddle. 'Otherwise I will be shamed. Not worthy to bear my father's good name.'

Brick was nonplussed. There was no answer to that. He held up his hands in capitulation.

'OK, partner.' He sighed in resigned acceptance of the inevitable. 'You got me there.' Then in a more sombre tone he added, 'You be extra vigilant. Remember, I will have to answer to your sister should anything happen to prevent your safe return.'

Consuela gripped his hand tightly. He could feel the contours of her taut body trembling with suppressed anxiety. A single tear etched a path down her left cheek.

But she remained silent. Her brother was right. Even though she dreaded the possible outcome, the girl respected his decision. This was *machismo*: the glorification of male superiority to which all Mexicans adhered unto death.

Wink nodded his understanding, nudging the black towards the looming rocky enclave.

Lengthening shadows of approaching night were enveloping the arid tract where the three riders had made camp when Wink eventually returned. He had the good sense to make a degree of noise on his approach so as not to precipitate any defensive gunfire.

'Halloo the camp,' he called out. Brick had instilled this form of address into the young Mexican after he had almost ventilated the boy's hide following his dramatic rescue from the Rocking Chair rannies.

'Lone rider coming in.'

The others quickly gathered round, eager to hear the boy's report.

'What you found, boy?' snapped Sackett.

All eyes focused on the drained horseman. He was exhausted.

'Give the boy chance to recover,' counselled his sister, helping Wink dismount. 'He dead on feet. Need rest.'

'And there ain't nothing we can do before daybreak,' agreed Brick, handing his partner a mug of coffee which the boy sipped gratefully.

The minutes dragged slowly as the boy recovered his wits.

It was Joe Sackett who was chafing most at the bit.

'Don't keep us in suspense, boy,' he said. 'What did you find out?'

'Wagon hidden inside a cave up in rocks.' Wink waved an arm vaguely in the direction of the surging hills, their serrated rims now reduced to grey lumps etched starkly against the flaming western sky. 'But nobody there. Gang has gone but have left guns on wagon.'

Brick's craggy features crinkled in thought.

'They must be aiming to set up a powwow with Manganellis,' he concluded, while staring rigidly into the dancing flames of the campfire. His brow furrowed as an idea began to take shape. The others watched, and waited.

He turned to Consuela.

'At first light I want you to return along our back trail. That way you ought to meet up with Buckweed Jackson and any other ranchers he's managed to persuade into backing the cause. We'll head up into the hills to this cave and keep guard over the guns.

If the gang return afore you and Buckweed then . . . ' That was something they'd have to face when the time came.

In truth he wanted the girl out of harm's way. Those skunks could return at any time with Maganellis and his bunch of renegades. He was just relieved that she had not voiced any objection to the task.

'You keep out of sight,' the Mexican girl responded. 'Too many of them. Not worth getting killed over.'

Brick chewed worriedly on his lower lip. A curt nod was his sole response.

The false dawn had barely elbowed aside the leaden blanket of night when Brick bade farewell to Consuela. The pair clung to each other like limpets. Only the imminent arrival of the daybreak's golden glow forced them apart. She kissed him tenderly on the lips. Her touch burnt like a hot flame. It made him tingle all over, sending shivers down his spine.

'Take care, *mi amante*,' whispered

173

the girl in his ear. 'And Pepe also. He needs your guidance more than he is willing to admit.'

'Come back *muy pronto*,' murmured the diffident man. 'I will count the minutes.' Unused to tendering such endearments, he felt somewhat abashed, awkward at having to reveal his innermost feelings.

Consuela's parting piece of advice was of a more pragmatic nature.

'Keep sharp eye on Joe Sackett', she murmured, the words barely above a muted whisper. 'He is close to limit. Like to go off rails. I have seen it happen many times to men who have lost everything. They lose will to live.'

Brick glanced across at the grizzled old rancher. His eyes were red-rimmed and staring, imbued with a wild, almost manic glaze.

'I'd noticed he was getting a little edgy and bad-tempered,' commented Brick. 'But I never figured he was going crazy.'

A quick peck on the cheek followed.

Then she was gone, her hazy outline disappearing into the gloom of early morning. It was a chastening moment for the young man.

12

Surprise at Mesilla Point

The sun was well above the eastern rim of the Pyramids when Consuela rounded a blunt-edged chunk of sandstone known as Mesilla Point. Jutting out from the main buttress of a prominent outcrop, it guarded the entrance to Palomas Canyon. Desiccated stands of mesquite blended with the grey-green creosote bushes that struggled to survive in this barren wilderness.

Rose-tinted aspirations concerning Brick Shaftoe occupied prime position in Consuela's thoughts. All she could think of was that last kiss. In consequence, her attention was far removed from the immediate concern of her present circumstances. Otherwise she might have heeded the drumming of hoofs echoing off the harsh rock wall enclosing the tortuous canyon along which the trail wound.

As a result she galloped around the sharp bend straight into the path of Chuck Williams. Accompanying him were the six gunhands he had hired to protect the Rocking Chair in the event of the Apaches deciding to double-cross him. Bareknuckle Beesley rode on his left side with Jug Lassiter and Dutch Eddie tailing behind.

Lassiter scowled. Hate-filled eyes bored into the bodyguard's broad back.

By his reckoning, he deserved to be top dog in this outfit, not playing second fiddle to that lumbering ox. Once they had been paid off for this final job, he would fix that critter permanently. Dutch Eddie sensed his buddy's loathing, but had no wish to become embroiled in some pointless feud. Behind Lassiter rode Frank Calder with his ever-present sidekick, Mac Doolin. Denver Blue brought up the rear.

Of the hired gunslingers, only Billy Gibbs was missing. His leg was healing fine but was still not up to the rigours of a protracted ride at pace. Instead, two days before he had been sent to inform Manganellis about the place where the sale would take place. The Indian chief was holed up in a secret canyon deep within the heart of the Hidalgo Pyramids. Crafty as a desert fox, he had made certain his camp was located on the Mexican side of the border, safe from any incursion by government forces.

The rest of the Rocking Chair crew were back at the ranch. They were all regular cow hands who knew nothing about the boss's surreptitious activities.

The abrupt meeting on the trail was as much a surprise to the Rocking Chair boys as it was to Consuela. Her horse reared up on its hind legs, tumbling her out of the saddle. The breath was knocked from her body as she landed with a thud on the hard ground.

Williams was the first to react to the sudden encounter.

'So what have we here?' he announced to the startled riders, whose own mounts were milling about in confusion.

'Looks like that feisty Mex dame from the hospital in Brass Neck.' Jug Lassiter nudged his horse to the front. He leaned over the bay's head, peering down at the stunned girl. His gnarled features bunched up into a wary grimace of mistrust. 'How come you're wanderin' alone in this god-forsaken wasteland, girl?' he snarled.

Consuela had been paralysed into silence through fear and the hard fall rather than any desire to thwart the gun-runners.

Williams quickly dismounted.

'You heard the man,' he snapped, grabbing her long flowing hair. 'No woman in her right mind would be out here riding solo. You'd best spill the beans else Jug here will be more'n pleased to dig the truth out of that pretty little hide of your'n.'

Lassiter removed a large Bowie knife from the hide sheath attached to his belt. Its lethal ten-inch blade glinted in the early morning sun.

Another gunslinger now stepped forward.

'Reckon I got the answer to that, boss,' butted in Frank Calder. Not the sharpest knife in the drawer, Calder nonetheless had offered some good ideas on previous occasions.

'Let's have it then, Frank,' said Williams evenly.

Calder nudged his mount forward. 'This gal was comin' down the trail from the same direction in which we're headed.'

'We know that, turkey,' sniped Lassiter.

'Then maybe you realize that, like as not, she's comin' from the cave.' Calder's acerbic reply bit deep into the gunslinger's brittle riposte. 'This girl must be in cahoots with the small ranchers and somehow they've found out where we've stashed the guns.'

'That right, girl?' rasped Williams shaking her roughly.

Consuela spat out her derision. 'Captive Indian spilled beans. Brick Shaftoe too good for likes of you.'

Denver Blue stepped up, expressing what they all now realized.

'Ain't that the same dude that gunned down Jinglebob?'

'That guy leads a charmed life,' observed Mac Doolin. 'How did the slippery critter escape from that noose?'

'Don't matter none any more,' snapped Williams, chewing on a dead cigar. 'Now that we do know, it also figures they'll be lyin' in wait for us.'

A sombre mood settled over the gathering.

Lassiter was the first to react. He jabbed the razor-edged blade against the girl's neck.

'Is that right, gal?' he growled. 'Is your boyfriend up there now?'

Consuela bit her lip. Even though she was terrified, her obstinate streak asserted itself. A touch of red flushed the girl's smooth cheeks as fear gave way to intense anger. Harsh laughter, brittle and sour, poured scorn on to the hovering gunmen.

'And he not alone,' she howled. 'Joe Sackett and my brother there also. You no get guns now that my man has whip hand.'

It was left to Bareknuckle Beesley to voice their dismay.

'What we gonna do, boss?'

Williams's face split into a broad grin.

'The answer's been thrust right into our laps, boys.' He chuckled mirthlessly. After admitting that she and Brick Shaftoe were entwined, Consuela had inadvertently supplied a way out of the gang's difficulty. 'This here Mex gal is our guarantee.'

Five puzzled faces stared back at him. Only Frank Calder had caught on. 'You mean that we trade her for the guns,' he said.

'You hit the nail on the head there, Frank.' Williams grinned. 'No way will that guy Shaftoe risk the girl's life to save a wagon full of rifles.'

Consuela's face dropped as she realized her error of judgement.

Hands tied securely, she was bundled on to her horse. Uttering a yip of triumph, the Rocking Chair boss led his men south towards the inevitable confrontation. It was a situation he would have preferred to avoid. But with the Mexican girl in tow, he was satisfied that all the cards were now stacked in his favour.

There was no way that Chuck Williams was going to be outwitted by a bunch of small-time cattlemen. But he knew that recovering the guns after the exchange was not the end of the matter. Brick Shaftoe and his buddies were bound to follow and await their chance to turn the tables before he had the chance to do a deal with Maganellis. His teeth ground in fury, knuckles blanching white as he gripped the butt of his hogleg.

They had to be stopped.

A hint of a smile cracked his rigid features. Maybe he had an ace up his sleeve.

He signalled for Jug Lassiter to join him up front.

'Got a mighty important job for you, Jug,' he muttered in a conspiratorial whisper. This was for the burly tough's ears only.

Lassiter's big flappers pricked up, waving like two Independence banners. This was what he wanted, to be the boss's right-hand man. The guy who did the business.

'Yeah, boss?' came the eager reply.

'Listen up good.'

★ ★ ★

'OK, boys,' announced Williams later that afternoon. 'This is where we leave the horses. The last half-mile is on foot.'

The gang, along with their ransom victim, were hidden behind a low bluff. Williams knew the terrain intimately, having brought previous shipments over the border. His intention was to come at the cave from behind, knowing that the frontal approaches would be under observation. No sense giving the bastards anything easy to shoot at, even if he was holding a royal flush.

'Check your guns and keep your eyes peeled,' Williams ordered his men. 'And you're in charge of the girl,' he said, addressing Dutch Eddie whose hand was still giving him some trouble. 'Keep her on a tight rein. Let her escape and you're dogmeat, savvy?'

The brittle threat brought a stammered response from the bulky gunslinger.

'S-sure th-thing, boss. You can count on me.'

Williams led the way along a dried-up arroyo that gently meandered up into the hill country. The high banks effectively prevented any eagle-eyed guards from spotting them. The hard bed of the arroyo made the going easier.

A half-hour later they had crested

the rocky slopes. Williams quickly positioned his men in the rocks surrounding the flat shelf beyond which was the entrance to the cave.

Of those who had commandeered the vital supplies of rifles, there was no sign. Shaftoe and his compatriots were clearly taking no chances of being caught unawares.

'You jaspers in the cave,' shouted Williams. 'Me and the boys have got you surrounded on all sides. There ain't no way out. Give up the guns and you can go free. You got my word on it. What d'yuh say?'

Only the low sigh of a desert breeze broke the heavy silence.

'No use tryin' to act tough, Shaftoe,' rasped the diminutive ranch boss. 'I know you're in there. Just be sensible and no one will get hurt.'

The deep, cough of a long rifle bounced off the back wall of the cliff face.

'Goddamnit!'

The startled yelp came from Bareknuckle Beesley, whose grey hat flew into the air. Two more well-placed shots sent it spinning away to settle in the branches of a palo verde tree.

'Next shot will take his head off,' was the curt response to the gang leader's suggestion. 'I'd trust a hungry sidewinder a sight more'n a skunk like you.'

Williams emitted a rabid snarl of anger. He signalled for Dutch to bring the girl up front. A brutal push sent her sprawling into the open at the end of the lariat.

'Now who's holdin' all the aces, mulehead?' A harsh guffaw was accompanied by a sharp tug on the rope, which jerked the girl off her feet.

Inside the cave, Brick stiffened. He lurched forward, a red mist of fury clouding his judgement.

'Easy, boy,' cautioned Joe Sackett. 'At least she's still alive. They wanna make an exchange. That's for sure.' His voice was hoarse, a raspy catch in his throat making it shake.

Although the apparent calm masked

an inner turmoil, Sackett had reached breaking point.

'Now you know I mean business, this is what happens,' declared the gang boss. His brisk tone suggested that he would brook no debate on the matter. 'One of you drive the wagon out of the cave along with your horses. That way you won't be tempted to follow after us. Got that?' He didn't wait for a reply. 'Then back off. I'll bring the girl down and drive the wagon off at a walk while she joins you fellas. That way you got the drop on me. And my boys have got her in their sights.' He finished with an attempt to lighten the tense atmosphere. 'Not that either of us wants to see any bloodshed, do we?'

'What d'yuh reckon?' Brick asked the old rancher.

Sackett shook his head. 'I don't see that we have any choice. The critter's got us trapped in here.'

Brick nodded. 'And he wouldn't bat an eyelid about killing Consuela.' He turned away to voice his reply. 'OK, mister, you got yourself a deal,' he hollered from a position behind the wagon. 'Just make darned sure you don't pull a fast one. I'm a crack shot as you just discovered.'

'Don't worry none, mister,' replied Williams. 'All we want are the guns.'

Brick hauled himself up on to the wagon and gently urged the horses into motion. Wink had tied their own mounts to the rear. He paused at the entrance to make certain that the Rocking Chair boss was keeping his side of the bargain.

The little man had a gun jammed into Consuela's back. She looked dishevelled and frightened, but otherwise appeared to be unharmed.

The wagon lurched out into the open and slowly trundled towards the centre of the open ground. Eyes fixed on the advancing duo, Brick alighted before backing off the way he had come. Bright sunlight reflected off the metal from at least three rifles hidden in the rocks overlooking the level shelf.

Williams stepped up on to the wagon and seated himself, the leathers firmly gripped in his left hand. His right still held the lariat secured around the girl's waist. 'When I release you, just walk over there nice and slow like,' he hissed. 'Make a dash for it and my boys'll gun you down.'

Then he cut the rope and gently eased the wagon team forward towards the gap in the circle of enclosing rocks.

Witnessing the lowlife cause of all his distress making his escape was too much for Joe Sackett. Something snapped inside his head. A grey curtain descended over his distorted brain. Any thoughts akin to rational decision-making were abandoned. A thunderous growl erupted from deep within his very soul. He dashed out into the open emptying his six-shooter at the back of the disappearing wagon driver.

Cock and fire!
Cock and fire!

There was no attempt to aim the pistol. He managed to get off only three shots before the hidden rifles chopped him down. An ear-shattering blast ripped across the shelf as the shredded body leapt and danced to the devil's tune. Blood poured from at least a dozen bullet wounds; they quickly stained the sand a dark brown.

In the nerve-tingling silence that followed, Sackett's punctured corpse twitched involuntarily before it lay still. And not one of his own shots had found the target.

The change in circumstances had all happened so quickly that no form of retaliation had been possible. Brick was stunned by the sudden breakdown of the old rancher. But at least Consuela was safe. The three survivors retreated from the exposed entrance to the cave. In the gloom at the back of the cave, Brick hugged the girl to his chest, running his hands through her long black hair.

'Thank the Lord you are safe,' he murmured into her ear. At the same time, tear-filled eyes were fixed on to the shattered corpse of his *compadre* lying splayed out in the open.

A harsh laugh broke into the tense atmosphere.

'Crazy bastard should have had more sense,' spat the re-energized gang boss. 'Nobody gets the better of Chuck Williams. You'd be well advised to heed that, Shaftoe. Try to come after us and you'll suffer the same fate.'

Brick grabbed a hold of his rifle and jammed it into his shoulder. But there was no target. Williams had ducked down in the wagon bed behind the boxes of rifles. The team carried on at a slow walk as if nothing untoward had happened.

'So long, jackasses!'

13

Manganellis Takes A Hand

A scorpion accelerated across the broad entrance to the cave, its deadly stinger probing the air for signs of prey. Outside, a hawk hovered in the azure sky. Suddenly it plunged like a stone, scooping up a horned toad that had been careless enough to show its head.

Death comes in many forms. And Brick Shaftoe was reminded of the bleak situation in which he and his *compadres* now found themselves. Alone and afoot miles from the nearest habitation.

Scanning the chaotic spread of rocks and boulders beyond the shelf, he noted that the glint from rifle barrels had disappeared. The gang were on the move, clearly anxious to conclude their business with Maganellis and head south into Mexico. Now that his gun-running scheme had been rumbled, Williams would not want to linger on American soil. Much better to find sanctuary in Mexico where he could regroup.

Brick's face set in a steely resolve as he emerged from the safe haven of the cave. He was determined to stick around and be ready when the varmint raised his festering head again in the future. As he surely would. Skunks like Williams were like flies on a dung heap. They never went away.

Brick soon discovered that only two half-full canteens of water were left together with a few sticks of jerked beef to chew on. It was not much for three of them, but would have to do until they could reach the nearest trading post at Big Hatchet.

Just as they were setting off, the bleak conclusion regarding the gun-runners intentions was brought starkly into focus.

'Stay where you are!' The blunt command slammed into their backs.

'And don't turn around!'

Brick cursed aloud. Williams had played them for suckers.

A brittle guffaw followed as the ratcheting of a half-dozen handguns sliced through the fetid air.

'Now unbuckle them gunbelts nice and slow.'

Brick briefly considered drawing his gun. But there were too many of them. And Consuela would like as not be killed. He couldn't take that chance. The belt hit the ground with a dull thud.

'Think I'd leave you buzzards to make trouble for me?' snarled Williams.

'Let the girl and her brother go,' pleaded Brick. 'It's me you want.'

Williams snickered.

'Sorry, fella. I don't cotton to leavin' any loose ends.' A brief pause followed when time hung heavy over the bleak landscape. Then. 'Let 'em have it, boys.'

But before the shattering blast of discharged six-gun lead dispatched the three comrades to the great beyond, the high-pitched prattle of Indian voices intervened. The buzz of loosed arrows was followed by a series of panicked howls.

Brick dropped to his knees, dragging Consuela down with him.

Swivelling round, his startled gaze fastened on to the tottering form of Chuck Williams. Arms raised, mouth hanging wide, the gun-runner swayed, then tumbled forward on to his face. There were six arrows protruding from his back. Panic gripped the rest of the crew. Beesley swung round and snapped off a couple of shots before meeting the same fate.

The others tried to escape. But there was nowhere to run. Doolin and Calder immediately threw down their weapons and raised their arms in surrender.

Only Denver Blue chose to continue the futile retaliation. But he was no match for the thirty Apache braves lining the crest of the ridge overlooking the rock shelf. And he too joined Williams and his bodyguard strumming with the Devil's handmaid.

The warrior chief sat his palomino with a supple grace. Opting for the traditional woven horse-blanket rather than a saddle, he gripped the animal's withers, allowing the fine animal to pick its own course down through the clutter of rocks hemming in the cave entrance. Dark eyes probed every nook and cranny behind which skulking bush-whackers could mount a counter-attack.

The worn leathery face had witnessed many suns rise and fall. Deep creases in profusion imbued the old chief with an appearance of eternal wisdom, so that many had come to regard him as a spirit in human form. As a result, he commanded profound respect. Few would have the nerve to challenge his decisions.

Maganellis brought his horse to a stop in front of the tall white man.

The disparate pair faced one another, each holding his adversary's chilly gaze. Neither was willing to back down, although Brick knew that he and his *amigos* were at the mercy of the Indians. One signal from the noble chief and they would be goners. In his right hand and lifted ready for throwing was a steel-tipped lance edged with eagle feathers. The grim, stony look, devoid of emotion, settled on to the surviving outlaws.

Their fate had been placed in the hands of the Indian agent.

Brick's face registered the fact that he was totally confounded. Why had the Apache chief killed the very men with whom he was supposedly doing business? Instead he appeared ready to spare the lives of his enemies.

He shook his head. Killing in cold blood was not his style. Arms raised, Brick gestured in sign language for the men to be released.

Manganellis lifted a questioning eyebrow. His heavily scored visage frowned in disapproval. The two gun-runners fell to their knees, pleading for mercy.

Then the lance was lowered.

'On your feet!' barked the Indian agent. 'This is your lucky day, boys. Just give thanks that I ain't the vindictive sort. And make the most of it. Cos if we meet up again, you're both dead meat.'

The reprieved gunslingers hurriedly stood up.

'Much obliged, mister,' burbled one of the pair. 'You won't be seein' us again. I guarantee it.'

'Then git, afore I change my mind.'

Not wishing to let go of their good fortune, the pair hustled over to their mounts and disappeared in a swirling cloud of dust.

Manganellis signalled for his braves to join him.

Brick stepped forward and made a suitable sign of greeting which the chief acknowledged. Then in the language of the Mescallero, he respectfully asked for an explanation.

It now occurred to Brick that perhaps Manganellis was shrewder, more cunning than Chuck Williams had given him credit for. Did the Apache want the guns for himself without having to hand over any remuneration? That seemed the obvious answer. So why spare the lives of those he had previously sought to terminate?

Only Manganellis could provide the solution to that poser.

The three survivors sat cross-legged facing the august Apache chieftain supported by his band of granite-faced warriors. Their drawn faces exhibited tense apprehension.

The chief snapped his fingers and instantly a long, smoking pipe was placed in his hands. It was intricately carved and strung with wild turkey feathers.

'First smoke pipe,' he intoned in a deep even drawl. 'Then talk.'

The ceremony took some time as each member of the tribe took his turn with the pipe. Brick was anxious to learn what the old chief was thinking. But there were no clues evident in the chiselled face.

After laying the pipe aside, Maganellis squared his shoulders and waited.

'Why, great chief of the Mescallero, do you smoke the pipe of peace with us, your sworn enemies?' Brick enquired. It was a direct question, straight and to the point. He had learned that this was the best way of dealing with Indian problems. Especially with those who had a grievance.

A wistful expression relaxed the stony features as Maganellis decided how best to respond.

* * *

After the raid on the white man's ranch, the chief needed time to recover from the bullet wound. He had lost much blood and was no longer in the first flush of youth. Injuries took longer to heal. But such was the respect accorded him by the Apache nation as first cousin of the renowned Cochise, that his word was law.

Summoning his elder braves,

Maganellis instructed them to go and bring in the bodies of those who had fallen in battle. Sometimes they were left on the field of battle. But the chief was concerned for his own son.

Horse Tail had not returned to their camp deep within the Hidalgo Pyramids. As the son of a chief he would be accorded the privilege of receiving full interment rites.

As the chief, Maganellis had to set an example of stoic resolve and determination in seeking revenge on the white eyes for betraying their promises. Treaties signed and sealed, guaranteeing the right of free and uninterrupted passage across their ancestral lands had been broken. Requests for fair treatment had been scorned by unscrupulous Indian agents seeking only to line their own pockets.

Maganellis had led a band of renegades on the rampage in retaliation. But their weapons were inferior to those in the hands of the white soldiers. Chuck Williams had offered to supply repeating rifles in exchange for gold.

Two moons had now passed since the last foray against the Bar S ranch. The raid had been specifically requested by the gunrunner. The Apache chief had not questioned the reasoning behind the white man's mania for ridding the valley of other ranchers. All the Indians were concerned with was venting their spleen against those they saw as usurpers of their tribal lands.

The pounding of hoofs broke into the chief's meditation. It was Cuchillo, the chief's young and reckless second-in-command. Maganellis needed to exert the full breadth of his authority to rein in his deputy's hotheaded attitude.

But Cuchillo had proved himself to be a strong and resolute fighter. The Indian brought his mount to a juddering halt in front of the chief's wikiup. Entering the low willow-framed structure, the Indian accorded his chief due respect by waiting for him to speak first.

'Did you find my son?' Maganellis

enquired, following the usual protracted greetings.

'You need to return with us to the ranch,' said Cuchillo, gratefully accepting a mug of fermented cactus milk.

The chief snorted impatiently. 'What do you mean by such words?'

'We could not move Horse Tail,' continued Cuchillo. 'His soul has already been carried into the afterlife. It would not be right. Only you, his father, can do that.'

'You mean that somebody has already conducted the funeral ceremony?'

Cuchillo nodded.

The chief's taciturn manner slipped. 'This I must see,' mewed the chief, climbing unsteadily to his feet.

The head wound was healing well.

The medicine man had first of all smeared it with a thick layer of bear grease. Being tough and hard to defeat, the bear was thought to heal its own wounds. The same properties were, therefore, considered suitable for alleviating human injuries. But its reek was worse than that of a skunk, and the rancid concoction had made the chief sick. As a result, he had washed the sticky mess off and now felt much improved.

So much for the power of the medicine man, whom he roundly condemned as a charlatan. But Maganellis still elected to wear the special headdress. Some ancient tribal practices become ingrained in the mind. And the war bonnet had been successful so far.

'Give your horse an hour to recover his stamina,' he said to Cuchillo. There was no mention of rest for the tired messenger. He was an Apache, and, therefore, expected to tolerate any amount of discomfort. 'Then we ride.'

It was a half-day trek back to the valley of the Bar S land.

Maganellis led his band of warriors into the empty corral. The blackened husk of the burnt-out ranch house presented a starkly brutal contrast to the pale orange of the towering butte to its rear.

'Take me to my son,' the chief commanded.

Cuchillo led the way round to the back of the root cellar.

It was as the Apache brave had recounted. And the manner in which Horse Tail's body had been treated received a look of approval from his father. The boy had died in battle. To an Apache there was no better way to make it into the afterlife. And his body had been accorded the full respect deserving of such a sacrifice.

Maganellis could only assume that at least one of the defenders had escaped and then returned at a later time. Why that person had then conferred the ultimate respect on his enemy was a mystery. Perhaps he would never learn the truth. But such a paleface had to be a man of extra special qualities, a man who would not hesitate to pursue and destroy his enemies.

It was a subdued group that returned

to the camp in the mountain hideaway to discover that one of the gunrunners had arrived with a vital message. It was Billy Gibbs, informing the tribe that the guns were ready for exchange. He gave directions to the cave before returning to the Rocking Chair.

★　★　★

Brick tried to affect an impassive regard. 'Why does the great Apache warrior kill only those who have the guns he needs?'

The old chief considered the question before replying. 'I, Maganellis, cousin to the great Apache warrior Cochise, watch from above.' His lance jabbed towards the skyline where back-up redskins stood watch. 'I see that you must be the one who honour the memory of my son Horse Tail, the one who showed great respect for his earthly form. I not let such action pass without returning favour. Why you do this thing, white man?'

Brick's right eyebrow lifted. 'I am Brickhill Shaftoe, the Indian agent for the south-west territories. My brother came to find out why the great Apache nation had risen up, and who were supplying them with firesticks. Many agents are evil men who seek only to rob the Indian. Brickhill Shaftoe not one of those. I want only what is best for Apache. Guns and killing are not the way forward.'

Drawing breath, he tried to fathom out what was going through the old guy's mind. It proved an impossible task. 'Many bluecoat soldiers will be sent by the Great Father in the East to punish Indians. Maganellis is wise. He knows these futile raids on innocent white ranchers are not the way forward. Show courage now by leading your braves back to the reservation.'

'We need more guns to continue struggle. Repeating rifles that will kill many white eyes.'

It was Cuchillo who had dared to interrupt.

A gasp went up from the assembled redmen. This was showing disrespect to the chief, challenging his authority.

Maganellis said nothing. His body stiffened as he turned slowly to spear the brazen warrior with a look of icy disdain. Many followed his example. But there were a few who silently offered support to the renegade Apache.

Then the chief's proud head drooped.

Age and a desire for peace were fast catching up with him.

The great warrior had indeed come to recognize the futility of endless raiding forays. Each time more men were lost and his force became weaker. Could the peace he yearned for ever be achieved by such means?

He carefully studied the contours of the white man's face. It possessed a tough, rugged appearance, yet seemed equally trustworthy and reliant; a face that promoted confidence, and whose owner could be relied on to deliver the goods. Perhaps the time had come to negotiate an honourable peace before it was too late.

A coyote howled its sad lament. Overhead, dark clouds were massing. In the distance a rumble of thunder heralded the imminent approach of the storm.

Nobody moved as the old chief cogitated. His craggy face remained set like stone, giving nothing away.

Then he spoke.

'Guns stay here.' Maganellis raised his lance. The wagon appeared, driven by one of the Indians. But of the saddle horses there was no sign. 'Now we go back to reservation.' Then to the Indian agent he issued a salutary warning. 'But if promises broken, expect much blood to flow.'

'You have my word, great chief,' Brick emphasized firmly. 'No more cheating or stealing of that which is rightfully due to the Apache.'

Without another word, the chief led his braves off the shelf and down on to the plains.

14

Hard Times

A huge sigh of relief escaped from between clenched teeth as Brick sank to the ground.

'Boy, that was a close thing,' he muttered sucking in lungfuls of precious oxygen. 'I never figured the old guy would back off like that.'

'It was your wise counsel that did it,' observed Consuela.

'And by giving chief's son a proper funeral.'

Wink's pertinent assertion brought a wistful aspect to the Indian agent's expression. 'Treat the Indian like a human being and he will meet you halfway,' he murmured.

Addressing Consuela he said, 'You fetch the horses. They can't have strayed far. Williams must have spooked them before he doubled back and got the drop on us. Wink and I will clean up Joe's body. Sooner we can get going the better. I won't rest easy until we've handed these guns over to the army at Fort Columbus. We can bury Joe next to his wife and daughter on our way to Brass Neck.'

After Consuela had departed, Brick voiced a more serious notion that had forced itself to the forefront of his thoughts.

'I'd bet my last silver dollar that Cuchillo is gonna cause a heap of trouble if'n he ain't stopped.' The comment emerged as they were reverently wrapping the bloodied corpse of Joe Sackett in a saddle blanket. 'The Agency will need to keep a close watch on his movements. And Maganellis will need all his strength and cunning to keep him in line.'

'Too late for that!'

The gruff retort was like a slap in the face. Brick swung round to face the speaker. Jug Lassiter stood there. Legs apart, ears twitching, a lurid smirk cracked the hard-bitten features. And with a cocked revolver in either hand, he clearly had the edge.

A brutal laugh erupted from his open maw on witnessing the startled expressions on the two helpless victims.

'Guess you forgot all about good ol' Jug, eh?' He took a step forward, jabbing the guns menacingly. 'Now hook out them shootin' irons nice and slow like, then toss 'em over here.'

Brick was cursing himself for a fool.

It was true. He had forgotten all about the jug-eared hardcase. And now, he and his young partner had been caught on the hop. They had little option but to comply.

'With all these boneheads out of the picture, I can sell off the guns to Cuchillo and keep all the dough for myself. All that stands between me and a life on easy street is you pair of donkeys.'

Lassiter was enjoying himself. He had been in private contact with the young renegade who was edging to take over from Maganellis.

In Cuchillo's view the aging chief was going soft and ought to step aside, allowing those with red blood in their veins to continue the fight against the white man's encroachment. Thus far he had kept such thoughts between a small number of like-minded braves. But the time for action was fast approaching.

Lassiter's jocularity was belied by thick lines of consternation furrowing his brow. A disquieting thought nudged at the gunrunner's devious brain. His original intention had been merely to shoot down this pair of meddling turkeys in cold blood and leave their corpses along with the rest for the scavenging coyotes to feast upon.

The problem was the wind direction. In the last half-hour, it had backed round to the north, ensuring that the departing Indians would be certain to hear the sound of gunfire. The old chief might well decide to change his mind and return for the guns. And Lassiter did not relish the alternative which was to hang around for another hour.

The gunman was impatient. He wanted to be away from this charnel house where the ripe odour of death now hung heavy in the air. His aim was to hide the guns in another cave he had sussed out until such time as he could return and make the trade with Cuchillo. And that might take a spell.

On the other hand . . .

A wicked gleam crept into his black eyes.

'Turn around!' he rapped, emphasizing the command with his guns.

'Just tell me one thing, Lassiter?'

'Yeah?'

'Was it you who killed my brother?'

'What d'you think?' was the blunt response. 'And now it's your turn.'

For a heavy-set outlaw, Lassiter was surprisingly nimble on his feet. Quick as a desert hare he leapt across the intervening few yards, and in the same fluid movement slammed the pistol barrel down hard on to the exposed head of the Indian agent.

Brick staggered forward. Stars erupted inside his skull. Desperately he attempted to claw himself back from the brink. But he was swimming against the tide. Confused and overwhelmed, his brain surrendered to the heavy blackness as he keeled over, and lay still.

Momentarily stunned by the brutal pistol-whipping of his partner, Wink then threw himself at the burly hardcase. Arms flailing like windmills, his whole being sought to pummel this son of Satan into the ground. Lassiter was the root cause of all the anguish he had suffered since that first encounter.

Small fists beat a tattoo on the thick-set torso. But to no avail. Lassiter was too strong. He easily shrugged off the greaser's puny efforts. At first he found it amusing.

'Come on, kid,' he laughed egging the boy on. 'You can do better'n this?'

But all too soon the entertaining diversion turned to intense vexation. A bestial growl hissing from the distorted mouth was accompanied by a volley of lurid epithets. He reached down and snatched a lethal Bowie knife from its boot sheath. Without scruple, he plunged the deadly blade into the boy's chest, flinging him aside like a discarded rag doll.

Blood sprang from the fatal wound. Wink grabbed at the hilt. His face screwed up in agony as he desperately tried to haul it free. But it was too late. He was dead before he hit the ground.

'Now it's your turn, mister,' snarled Lassiter. 'Not a quick death for you though. No sirree.' He chuckled with manic glee. 'Yours will be nice and slow.' His ugly face puckered in regret. 'Only pity is that I won't be around to enjoy the show.' The rabid grin disappeared as Lassiter aimed a savage kick at the prostrate body.

Then he went in search of the things he required.

Within a quarter-hour Brick was staked out on the far side of the shelf beside some rocks. The bushwhacker was prodding a stick into a crevice. Suddenly the tell-tale rattle brought a smile to his warped features.

'Come on out, fellas,' he warbled in a deranged voice, 'It's showtime.' Then he splashed some water on to the upturned face of the bound captive. 'Cain't have you missin' out on your own party now, can we?'

A strangled gurgle escaped from Brick's supine form.

'Won't be long now.'

But Lassiter was already hustling across to the wagon where the team of four were patiently waiting. He hopped up on to the bench seat and leathered them into motion. Soon he was out of sight, heading back in the direction of the San Luis pass.

It was another ten minutes before Consuela reappeared on the far side trailing two horses behind her own. The scene that met her anxious gaze barely registered at first. How could such a situation have occurred during the brief period she had been away? The Devil's

Kitchen could not display a more bloodcurdling tableau.

Her brother was splayed out in the sand. A startled look of dread was etched into the waxy features, a wicked knife protruding from his chest. Only one glance was necessary to convince the girl that Pepe Montoya was dead. Her gaze shifted to the far side of the shelf where Brick Shaftoe had been staked out. From this position, there was no telling whether or not he had met the same fate.

She sucked in a deep breath as a full-grown diamondback slithered out of a gap in the rocks. On sensing an imminent threat to its nest, the creature squirmed and twisted, its tail bones hammering out a discordant cacophany. The ugly mouth unhinged to reveal a pair of lethal fangs.

The moment of no return was at hand.

In the blink of an eye, the girl had whipped out the trusty Springfield from its saddle boot and jammed the rifle into her right shoulder. Without seeming to aim she fired. The roar of firing needle striking cartridge bounced off the surrounding rocks as black smoke poured from the long barrel.

The snake's lunging head burst asunder as the charge struck home. Blood and gore smeared the rock wall behind.

Consuela dashed across to her paramour. A groan escaped from his cracked lips. She breathed a sigh of relief. Unfastening the leather binding thongs she manhandled him away from the scene of death over to the mouth of the cave. There she dribbled water into the parched mouth.

'Who was it?' she asked. 'Who did this awful thing?'

'Lassiter,' came back the choked response. 'Got the drop on us, then slugged me out cold.' He gripped her arm tightly. 'How's Wink?'

The bowed head said it all.

'Then I gotta go after him.' Brick tried to lift himself but his head felt as though it had been kicked by a mule. He fell back, groaning.

'You no can do,' stressed the girl, dribbling more water into his mouth. 'Much too weak.' She peered around the grisly site. '*Mal hombre* has taken wagon. I follow and make him pay full price for guns . . . ' She paused, a lump constricting her throat, 'and Pepe's life.'

Brick was too feeble to object.

She left him propped up, back against a boulder with a pistol by his side.

Then she left. On passing the shattered body of her brother, the Angel of Mercy made the sign of the cross, whispering a few endearments before mounting up and spurring off down the main trail. This was the only route that a fully loaded wagon could have taken.

Leathering the horse unmercifully, she flew across the sagebrush plain, dodging between the clumps of chaparral. After ten minutes she spotted a cloud of dust some two miles ahead. It had to be Lassiter. A steely glint of triumph flushed out her pallid cheeks.

★ ★ ★

The single rifle shot echoing across the bleak wilderness was not lost on the Apache chief. But Maganellis gave no hint of having heard it. His blunt features remained immutable, his pace a steady canter as he continued leading the tribe in a northerly direction.

The rifle shot had not been ignored by Cuchillo, however. His rawboned head swung round towards the fading reverberation. Maybe this was the moment to make his play. Someone else could have grabbed those rifles? And they would be essential for creating more carnage among the hated settlers.

With a furtive sign to his co-conspirators, Cuchillo kneed his horse forward ahead of the rest. Fifty yards ahead he swung round blocking the trail and forcing the others to draw rein.

'What is this?' enquired Maganellis. 'Why you block path?'

'It is time for you to step down, old man,' Cuchillo called aloud so that everyone could hear. 'And let a true Apache carry on the fight against the white eyes.' Cuchillo raised his lance into the air in a challenge to the old chief's authority. 'Maganellis is like an old woman: too easily swayed towards the coward's way out.' He spat into the sand. 'Reservation is for old men and children, and those not fit to be Mescallero Apaches.'

The braves ranging behind their chief shifted uneasily.

This was the first time that a serious challenge had been made to usurp the great Maganellis. Such insults could not be issued without response.

For two long minutes the chief remained silent. Only the distant croaking of a bullfrog disturbed the tense stand-off.

Then it happened. Later, braves would shake their heads in disbelief. None of those present saw it happen. But it certainly did.

One moment the arrogant pretender was vying for the ultimate prestige, strutting like a proud peacock, the next he was lying in the sand with two arrow shafts in his heart.

Those behind the chief kneed their horses into a line facing the rebels. With notched bows, they drew back the string and aimed them at the small group of rebels.

Maganellis waved a dismissive hand towards the dead Indian.

'That is what happens to those who seek to go outside the laws laid down by the tribal council.' The chief spoke in a deliberately slow and measured tone. Flat and devoid of emotion, its effect was all the more telling. 'Others who choose that way will find they have embarked on a trail of tears. Make your choice, dogs.' His guttural delivery assumed a more sinister intonation. 'Rejoin your comrades, or join Cuchillo in the underworld.'

Heads bowed, the thoroughly chastened bunch slunk back into line. The uprising had been well and truely dispatched.

Maganellis snorted imperiously as the shamed Indians passed him, then raised his bow and pointed it north.

★ ★ ★

Jug Lassiter was feeling pleased with himself. All he had to do was secrete the guns in a hidden draw he had chanced upon, then get in touch with Cuchillo. The renegade had promised to pay in gold. And Lassiter would make sure he got top dollar for the cache. Then it was Mexico and a life of leisure with all those lovely *señoritas*.

His dreamy contemplation was cut short by the sharp crack of a rifle slug. Swivelling round on the hard seat, his screwed-up eyes scanned his back trail. Nothing. Surely that critter hadn't escaped his just deserts again.

He waited another five minutes. Then suddenly, a lone rider appeared on a low knoll, sitting astride a sorrel some 500 yards to the rear. Another shot rang out. A plume of dust fifty yards back indicated where it had landed.

The gunrunner uttered a disdainful laugh.

Way out of range.

That was when the mysterious pursuer removed her hat. Black hair streamed out, fanned by the desert wind.

The Mexican girl. Damn it! He'd forgotten about her.

Grabbing the Winchester carbine that lay in the wagon bed, Lassiter chambered a round into the breech. The girl nudged her mount further down the slope. Stepping down, Lassiter spread his legs wide for balance, and waited. He hugged the carbine to his shoulder, squinting down the barrel. Another twenty yards and you'll be in range, Lassiter muttered to himself.

Then the girl stopped. Just ten yards short of the effective range for a carbine. Lassiter wrinkled his nose in puzzlement. What was she up to?

With calculated ease, Consuela slid out of the saddle. She even waved at the mystified killer.

The deliberate tormenting of the gunrunner precipitated the desired reaction. He loosed off a couple of shots. But they fell short.

Bending down on one knee, Consuela thumbed a shell into the breech of the long-barreled Springfield. Shouldering the hunting rifle, she took careful aim, gently squeezing the trigger. The gun bucked against her shoulder.

Lassiter's hat flew into the air.

Repeating the process with practised efficiency, the next shot removed his left ear. A crimson fountain spurted from the ragged wound.

'Aaaaaagh!'

The howl of agony carried clearly across the desert floor. But the girl's face remained hard, relentless as she reloaded.

Lassiter clapped his bandanna to the bleeding mess and tried to reach cover behind the wagon. He never made it. The final shot caught him in the back of the neck. He went down like a sack of potatoes. Consuela knew instinctively that it had been a killing shot.

Slowly she remounted and pointed the horse down towards the wagon. Drawing up beside the prostrate corpse of the killer, her face displayed no emotion, no remorse for the taking of a human life. Neither elation nor anger. A foul deed had been avenged. It was the way things had always been.

She tied her own mount behind, climbed up on to the bench seat and turned the team around heading back towards the shelf. Buzzards circled overhead, their greedy eyes focused on the shattered corpse.

An hour later and the team of four were trundling slowly back through the Hidalgo Pyramids. Brick felt sufficiently recovered to ride up front. Wink's body lay next to that of Joe Sackett in the back, covered by a tarpaulin. No words had been uttered since Consuela's return. As if in a daze she had taken charge. Brick was content to give her free rein. It was all over. But would life ever be the same again?

After three hours a rising cloud of yellow dust could be seen ahead. Was it the Apaches returning to claim back the guns? Tense and expectant, the two riders held their breath.

As if in slow motion, a dozen high-crowned Stetsons poked through the hazy mist. It was Buckweed Jackson and the other cattlemen.

'Boy! Am I glad to see you, guys,' exclaimed the relieved rancher, reining up. 'We lost the trail aways back. Didn't know which direction you'd headed.' That was the moment when Jackson realized the others were missing. One look at the pair of gaunt faces and he knew something bad had happened. The query emerged as a tentative croak. 'Where's Joe and young Montoya?'

Brick swallowed, the ashen features self-explanatory as he slung a thumb to his rear.

'In the wagon beneath the tarp.'

Monk Reagan asked the next question, which was on all their lips. 'What in tarnation has happened?'

'It's a long story.' The gaunt, hollow-eyed expression on Brick's face discouraged any further discussion. This was not the time for explanations. All would be revealed in due course.

'One thing I managed to dig out of the sheriff last time I was in Brass Neck,' Jackson hurried on, 'was the reason Williams was so goldarned eager to get all the ranchers out of the valley.'

At this revelation he had Brick's undivided attention.

'Seems like the South Pacific Railroad were fixing to push a branch line through the town. Williams was hoping to get rich quick by selling them the land. But all this trouble with the Indians persuaded the company to follow the northern route through Lordsburg.'

'So all the killing was for nothing.'

The cheerless comment was received in numbed silence. The stunning implications required some digesting.

The group of riders hung back some way behind the wagon, providing a solemn escort as they headed north towards Fort Columbus. Jackson realized that the two survivors needed space, time to be alone with their thoughts.

Brick fingered the bandage swathing his throbbing head. It had been expertly applied by this Angel of Mercy, and the Indian agent knew he was in safe hands. And he was relishing the novel sensation. The girl's shoulder brushed his.

Then she turned and kissed him full on the lips, ignoring the astonished looks on the faces of their escort. Unexpectedly but no less welcome, the beneficiary responded warmly.

'It all over now, Brickhill Shaftoe,' Consuela whispered tenderly. 'Bad men gone. Justice done.'

The haggard face offered the hint of a smile as the man peered deep into the girl's hauntingly beautiful eyes.

'Maybe it's just beginning,' he murmured softly. Pausing, a crafty gleam animated his features. 'And once we have won back your inheritance, who knows where the trail might lead?'

THE END

We do hope that you have enjoyed reading this large print book.

Did you know that all of our titles are available for purchase?

We publish a wide range of high quality large print books including:
Romances, Mysteries, Classics
General Fiction
Non Fiction and Westerns

Special interest titles available in large print are:
The Little Oxford Dictionary
Music Book, Song Book
Hymn Book, Service Book

Also available from us courtesy of Oxford University Press:
Young Readers' Dictionary
(large print edition)
Young Readers' Thesaurus
(large print edition)

For further information or a free brochure, please contact us at:
Ulverscroft Large Print Books Ltd.,
The Green, Bradgate Road, Anstey,
Leicester, LE7 7FU, England.
Tel: (00 44) **0116 236 4325**
Fax: (00 44) **0116 234 0205**

Other titles in the
Linford Western Library:

VENGEANCE RIDES THE RIVER

Hugh Martin

The murder of Dave Lockhart's wife, by desperados who plague the Red River country of Texas, results in his desperate mission for revenge. Lockhart is no natural killer, but his quest for revenge becomes marked by murder, bullets and gun-smoke, and brings him face to face with deadly men. Then he meets Helen, who must overcome difficulties that few women ever face. Now she must teach Lockhart that there can be a world of difference between vengeance and justice . . .